House of Cards

Sin City Shard Chronicles

C.S. Kading & Tony Fuentes

SandDancer Publications

For English Teachers everywhere, who are brave enough
to try and teach the classics to rooms full of teenagers.
Thank you.

*...and we apologize for what we are about to do to The
Bard.*

Contents

A Disagreement

The table next to me exploded into a cloud of ice and splinters.

"That's not a very noble gesture, Your Grace!" I shouted across the room. The answer I received was a volley of razor-like ice spikes flung in my direction.

Just another typical Tuesday afternoon.

I ducked behind the doorway and pressed my back to the concrete wall.

"The changeling child is my teind, Shard Keeper, I will not relinquish him to you!" a melodious, if angry, voice yelled at me.

ShardKeeper. She'd invoked my title. Well, at least that meant she recognized it. That was better than most days.

"I can't let you keep him, Your Grace," I called back. Titles were important when dealing with the Fae. It showed an understanding of the established pecking order of things. A squire knew to bend the knee to the knight, who knew to bend their will to their Liege and understood the importance of following the word of their laird. There was order in the otherwise orderless Courts of the Fae-Kin ... as long as you followed the rules.

Tatiyana Scawen had been the Laird of Las Vegas for almost fifty years now. A fearsome creature, she emerged from a time when humanity believed in dreams becoming reality, crafting horrors and heroes.

And she was pissed.

"His mother GAVE him to me!" she cried. Another volley of ice spikes flew toward the doorway, followed by a gust of wind and sleet. The doorframe next to me became coated with ice rime. The floor became slick and frozen.

This was not going well.

"She was incarcerated at Florence McClure, Your Grace. That's outside your territory." Reason sometimes worked when tempers were high.

Tatiyana screamed a stream of obscenities in my direction.

Then again, maybe not this time.

Each of the ruling Kin claimed specific areas of the Vegas Valley and surrounding communities. Their people lived in those areas and, as expected, abided by the traditions as established within their cultures. But every now and again, one of the Kin dipped their wick into someone else's lamp oil, and shit like this happened.

"He can't have the child!" she roared.

Thunder cracked overhead.

Well, crap, now she was calling in air support. It was going to get worse before improving. Tatiyana was a weather witch among her people. She could command the seasons and their elements. Flowers bloomed in her footsteps, and lightning rained from the sky at her displeasure. Each Laird possessed its own magical arsenal. Her husband ... Consort, I corrected myself. They weren't married any longer but were still bound by Fae-Kin Oath as balance points. Her Consort, Oberon Elegast, was a master in the arts of charm and mass manipulation. His talents rivaled those of the ruling Hemophage Blood-Kin.

North Las Vegas was his territory, and the correctional facility was in North Las Vegas. The changeling child was born to an inmate three weeks ago. The mother, who recently transferred, whose release should have happened before the child's birth, but someone's paperwork delay postponed her freedom. Conjugal visitation had resulted in the child's conception when she was elsewhere, but the birth happened here. Incarceration facilities were not safe places - even for expectant mothers.

Oberon Elegast was a cold and calculating ass, but he took his Oaths and responsibilities to his Kin personally. The woman responsible for the Changeling's premature birth met an unfortunate, perhaps deserved, end. Such was the price of endangering one under His care. That act came with a price of its own. The Child, by Fae-Kin tradition, was His. It didn't matter what the mother had signed in the mundane Court. The expectation was for Tatiyana to relinquish the child.

And she was not having it.

The familiar sound of an incoming phone call bleeped in my Bluetooth wireless earbud. I reached up to tap it, answering it.

"Nice of you to join me, Malik."

I leaned, quickly assessing the room beyond the doorway. Ice flew at my head. I ducked back once more.

"I was on the train along The Strip, thank you very much. I couldn't just jump into the Library from car 34," Malik's deep baritone answered. His voice, flavored by years abroad, defied easy categorization.

"Sounds like an excuse to me," I teased. Calling Malik Salah the Librarian of the City did not give enough weight to what he actually did. He was a keeper of records, decipherer of tomes, a researcher of lost legends, and a damned good man.

"Ah yes, allow me to craft an excuse for not wanting to be surrounded by a wealth of lost knowledge on this cloudy Tuesday morning …" he answered. A loud crash of thunder and lightning sounded overhead, and crackling was heard across the airwaves. "Well, Her Grace sounds like she is in fine form today …"

"Less chatter, more answers, Malik!" I replied. I smelled ozone in the air and felt a tingle of electricity on my skin.

"Right! Tatiyana Scawen, ruling Laird of Las Vegas. Her books are pretty tight, Lyn."

The hair on my arms rose. I pushed away from the wall and metal. I knew what was coming next.

"She's gotta owe us something, Malik! I need it! NOW!" I shouted and threw myself onto the painted concrete floor, hoping the material would limit the conductivity of what she was about to throw at me.

The air crackled above me as a ball of electricity formed. It was a small round globe with strands and threads of dancing light shooting off it in multiple directions. Some threads reached out toward the metal beams overhead. I could feel the electricity buzzing all around me.

This was gonna suck so hard.

Sometimes the mind chose the most inopportune times to take trips down memory lane.

I wasn't always a Shard Keeper.

Ok, that point was up for some debate, depending on which faction you wanted to listen to. The point however was that I remembered when I had a normal life. Well, normal for a foster kid growing up in the system, I suppose.

Family hopping. Lack of food security. Carrying my belongings around in a trash bag and wondering if the family I was with was gonna be at least tolerable or if I was gonna end up having to earn my place in some weird-ass ranking system that only the other kids in the house knew? Ya. That was my normal.

That nuclear-family stuff you read about? That's some Disneyland-level fantasy.

I wanted it, just like every other kid. I dreamed of a room of my own whose door I didn't have to lock every night. Or have a whole dresser full of drawers that were mine. Adults who were more interested in being parents rather than just seeing how many kids they could keep in a house for the sake of their State Care checks? Ya. I wanted that.

Maybe the City chose me for this reason. Much like Sin City, I knew the truth hidden beneath the surface. And maybe because I understood the importance of taking a gamble.

Tamara Lyn Hunter. That was the name that was listed on my birth certificate. The authorities redacted my biological parents' names from my files. They were nowhere to be found. I'd looked. Fleeting memories were all I had of them. I remembered my mother's laugh, exuberant and rich and flavored with sass. She had long, dark hair, and when the sun hit it right, you could see hints of red woven through the strands. Her skin was the color of creamed coffee. My father was a big man. Though seen through the eyes of a child, it was hard to know exactly how big he really had been and how distorted the memories were. He had black hair that he wore in a long braid down the middle of his back and a wide handlebar mustache. His features reminded me a little of the King of Venice Beach - Danny Trejo.

There was an accident when I was about six. Or that was what I had been told. I went to stay with an aunt. That didn't last long. Child Protective got involved before I was seven, and I was family hopping by age eight. Already too old for most families looking to adopt.

All the horror stories you hear about kids that get lost in the system? Ya, they're all true. You don't want them to be. You keep hoping that maybe you will be the one that escapes it all. But in the end, you just end up a statistic. Like everything else in the City, it's a numbers game.

I spent eight years being traded around between houses and schools before I met Dean Franklin. He was a counselor at Las Vegas High. Home of the Wildcats. As far as public schools went, it wasn't so bad. Dean was the only dude on the Counselor Staff. The rest were all women.

He was a middle-aged white guy, with a military-style buzz cut and bright blue eyes. Cigars, Aqua Velva, and a smile that stopped a room. He counseled students whose last names were G - L, so I got assigned to him. The first time I walked into his office, I remember thinking that this was going to be a terrible experience. One more adult trying to help me "find my way" and keep me from "ending up in jail." But he wasn't like that. He actually listened. When we met, he let me decide if the door stayed open or closed. He paid attention when I expressed an interest in certain classes and wrote the exceptions to get me into those classes. Where my foster parents dropped the ball, Dean picked it up.

He kept weird hours for a counselor, but no one seemed to question it. If the theatre kids were rehearsing, or the athletes were practicing, his office would be open. I look back at it now and understand there was more to it, but it still meant a lot to me.

When I graduated from High School, he gave me the name and phone number of someone who had a job already lined up for me. It wasn't changing sheets in a hotel or emptying trash cans for some office building.

It was a cat cafe.

I alternated between learning basic animal care, helping folks who were interested in adopting rescued animals, setting up events for the Cafe, and learning how to be a barista. I learned the business. I learned to account. I learned how to network.

I learned people.

This skill would be more valuable than anything else I learned.

Unfortunately, good as my people skills were, Tatiyana still threw lightening at me.

Tiny bolts of electricity shot past me, drawn to the doorway and the beams overhead. I could smell ozone and fried circuitry. If she couldn't get to me, Tatiyana was going to set the building on fire. Laying there in the middle of a concrete walkway, pondering whether the Las Vegas Laird was going to electrocute me or burn me to death, I wondered if learning a combat skill might not have been a better choice.

Chicks Dig Scars

"Botham!" Malik's voice shouted through the phone in a Eureka moment. "Tatiyana still has an outstanding debt to us for Botham!"

"Pretty sure that happened when she was still with Oberon, Malik. I think His nibs owns that one ... technically," I replied.

Fae-Kin always seemed to repeat the same pranks, offenses, and actions that had worked for generations past. The difference is that nowadays, drugging someone's drink often landed you in jail besides whatever other penalties they might suffer in their own Court. Nicky Botham had been in the wrong place at the wrong time one night. She ended up the target of a fight between Oberon and Tatiyana when they were in the middle of falling out with each other.

Nicky was a hell of a mechanic and had carried a torch for the Laird for years. She happily worked on every piece of machinery Tatiyana sent her and cut her a sweet deal for it, too. One night, Tatiyana had shown up to check on a project herself. Alone. When the Laird propositioned Nicky, the mechanic did not say no. Broke Nicky's heart when she found out it was because of Oberon's magic.

The previous Shard Keeper had pulled Nicky out of a tub, wrapped her wrists, and gotten her the help she needed. Made the Fae-Kin fix the books.

Nicky remembered little of the whole incident, thankfully. But there were days when she would look wistfully toward the Strip. I knew she was thinking of the Laird and that stolen moment that neither of them should have had.

The smell of burning circuitry increased, coupled with smoke. Lights flashed suddenly and overhead sprinklers cut in. Water fell from the pipes overhead, flooding the area.

Water on the concrete.

Electricity overhead.

Two great things that were not great together. I rolled to the side and jumped to my feet.

"Fuck, fuck, fuck!"

I headed for the open door as quickly as my booted feet could carry me.

"Run, little rabbit!" A melodious cackle followed me out of the building. I hit the door, shoving it open, just as a ribbon of blue and white electricity touched the puddle of water that my foot was in.

The sharp burning that came with hot and cold bit into me... It started at my foot and clawed its way up my leg. My muscles spasmed and jerked and suddenly I was falling forward. There was so much pain my body and mind couldn't keep up.

And then darkness.

There were some cool things about being a Shard Keeper that I had learned in my years holding the position.

The first was - you couldn't become a Blood-Kin, also known as a Vampire. Something in the blood just rejected the transference of the Hemophage virus. The same property that prevented a Keeper from becoming Blood-Kin also prevented the various ... and there were many ... Shifter-kin from infecting you. Sounds pretty cool, huh? It certainly had its benefits. I also had limited resistance to Fae-Kin magic. Limited meant things like charms and body-warping magics. It did not, however, prevent the natural properties of electricity from doing what it would normally do to my body.

Malik carefully cut the boot off my foot and peeled it back. The flesh beneath was red and blistered. A spider-web of angry marks ran up the length of my leg. It looked very much like a lightning bolt.

"HP be jealous of that." Malik chuckled a little as he admired the mark.

"At least he had magic to fight with in the books." I groaned a little and shifted so I could get a better look at the injury. My leg looked like I had pulled it out of a pit bar-b-cue.

"Have no fear, mon frere, I got you," Malik replied and held out his hands over my red and blistered leg. He closed his amber eyes, breathed, and muttered in a language I didn't understand. I felt the healing magic course through my body, skillfully knitting and pearling the damaged and broken cells back together.

Magic was not as unusual as I had been raised to believe. As evidenced by the existence of Bood-Kin, Shifter-Kin, and Fae-Kin - the supernatural was alive and well and occupied places in everyday life. They weren't alone, either. There were others.

So. Many. Others.

Once I started digging into the legends and lore of things, the existence of regular-joe-human was kinda rare. Even then, the odds were often high that regular-joe-human was probably related to one of the Kin types, or under their protection. On the upside, regular-joe-human usually weren't involved in anything involving most of the Kin. On the downside, that often meant that many Kin felt like they could do whatever the hell they wanted and never get caught.

Where mankind settled, the Kin appeared. They were both the blessing and curse of human dreams, ambitions, desires, and fears. Humanity grew, and so did the Kin. Wars had been fought for millennia between the Kin across the entire world in various attempts to leverage control. Battles and bloodshed led to the creation of the Shard Keepers, according to tomes. Even among the Keepers, the true origins of what we were were hotly debated. I honestly don't think any of us really know where the first Shard emerged or why.

What we could all agree on were three things: Shard Keepers were immune to almost all the supernatural gifts, magic, powers, and curses the Kin wielded. There was only one Shard Keeper ever-present in an area with a dense human population. Killing a Shard Keeper often led to bad things happening to the city itself.

The fall of Palenque in the Yucatan was directly attributed to one of the Shifter-Kin assassinating the Keeper. The fallout destroyed the city. The fields became barren, and the people were forced to abandon the area.

Thonis-Heracleion? Fell into the sea because the Keeper got caught in the crossfire between the Spirit-Kin and Blood-Kin there. Poison still kills us. Go figure.

Trellech? That was mostly because of human wars and plague, but the Kin were involved and none of them lifted a magic-coated finger to save the Keeper of the most densely populated city in ancient Wales. Where is it now? Buried under a field somewhere.

My leg had stopped throbbing and now looked less like a split pork roast and more like my calf. The spider-web of red still danced up the length of my calf and thigh, like a huge tattoo.

"That's gonna leave a mark," I commented.

Malik nodded. "Indeed. Not enough to kill you, but certainly enough to make a point."

Keepers weren't immortal. Not by any stretch. We lived, loved, married, had children, and eventually died. Some lived longer lives than others; but there was no curse of longevity among us, that was certain.

If one wanted to romanticize it, Shard Keepers were the physical embodiment of the soul of the City. Kill the Keeper. Kill the City. Kin, generally speaking, didn't want to kill their cities. To borrow from Carlin, it's where they kept their stuff, and Kin loved collecting stuff.

So, kill us? Not usually. Try to manipulate and bully us into doing what they wanted?

All the fucking time.

In Walked Trouble

A lot of Kin thought that being a Keeper was some romantic, all-powerful experience. I suppose some Keepers might have had that sort of relationship with their Shards. I'm pretty sure the Keeper of say, Venice had a very different relationship with their city-soul than the Keeper of Boston. Venice was also several hundred years older and probably had their shit worked out. I often wondered if the Keepers of the Old World Cities looked at the Keepers of the New World and just wanted to send us all to bed with a Hot Toddy or a spanking.

As it had been explained to me, the soul of the city needed a house to walk around in. Someone that would be an outward representation of what the City was - at that moment. I don't know why, man, it's just a thing. They don't pay me to ask that kind of question. Do you want a deep philosophical dialog on the subject? Go talk to Oxford. I'm pretty sure he gets off on those discussions.

Vegas in the 1950s and 1960s? He looked a lot like he belonged in the Rat Pack. Fingers in everybody's criminal pies, girl on both arms. He was also a businessman and a builder. He knew people, and he knew money, and he worked them both. The Kin of Vegas under that Keeper didn't even think of trying to step out of line, or they ended up being built into the foundation of one of the many casinos on the Strip.

Turn of the Century Keeper was a tech-guru, PR professional, and investor. Bigger, bolder, braver. He balanced appointments and ledgers as nobody else could. He was connected, and he kept those connections sharp and current. I think he may have been made of money.

I remember the afternoon Dean walked me into his office. I did not know why I was going to see the man who managed the assets of the wealthiest casino investor in the City. I figured it was to ask for a charity donation for the cafe. Dean told me to "just be yourself" and not worry about trying to impress anyone. I wore my black suit pants and a red business corset shirt. I remember wearing this chunky white necklace and big earrings I had for special occasions. Dean chuckled a little when he saw me. I punched him in the shoulder.

I am certain that August Murr had been a handsome man in his youth. Now, older, wealthier, and wiser, he seemed a stereotypical American businessman. His suit was sharp, his eyes were clear. He smelled like a man who had grown accustomed to smoking in his office before ordinances forced him to stop. I remember seeing a heavy glass ashtray on his dark wood desk. It was filled with Jolly Rancher candy. His face was stretched from bad plastic surgery. But despite his age and his rancor, there was something inherently powerful about him I could not deny.

"Yer shittin me, Frank. Her?" the old man said as he looked at me. His distaste was obvious. I'd seen it before ... every time I walked into an interview for something that wasn't housekeeping.

"Times change, Auggie," Dean replied.

I looked between the two older men. There was something between them. I didn't know what it was, and at that moment in time, I didn't care.

"Does she even know why she's here?" Murr asked.

I bristled at the dismissive manner in which Murr spoke about me, instead of to me.

"SHE came as a favor to a friend," I replied. I looked up at Dean and shook my head. "I'm sorry, Dean, I don't know what we need from this guy, but we can get it somewhere else." I turned and headed for the door.

The charming assistant behind the desk outside the door stood as I walked out. His amber eyes filled with concern as he looked back over my shoulder and then back at me.

"Uh ... show you out, Miss Hunter?" he offered. The nameplate on his desk read "Malik Salah." I paused at his voice.

"I can find my way, but if you want to validate this, it will help." I pulled my parking ticket out of my phone wallet.

"Sure thing." He nodded with an uncomfortable smile as he reached into his desk and pulled out a stamp and pressed it to the ticket. I took it back from him and tucked it into my case.

"Hey, uh. Lemme walk you out."

"I don't need an escort."

"Huh? Oh No. I'm pretty sure you don't. I just ..." He dropped his voice and leaned in a little. "I just want to make sure you are ok, ya know? Murr can be... a bit much."

I paused and regarded the amber-eyed man. I shrugged. "Sure. Whatever. Knock your socks off, Superman."

He smiled at the comment and stepped away from his desk. "I much prefer Spiderman, if we are to be making comparisons... the elevation of the Everyman to superhuman standing in literature and culture has been a personal study of mine..."

Four years later, he was still a nerd.

"I checked Tatiyana's books. She has a few favors on file that we could pull in if needed to get her to transfer custody, but they are huge favors or a bunch of little ones that we might have to use to pull weight," Malik said. His glasses perched on the end of his nose as he peered through the ledger. Maintaining peace within a city was one duty of the Shard Keeper. In theory, if the Keeper was involved, it showed a need to keep the City alive. An obscure and antiquated system of favors was often used to accomplish this. Legends abounded throughout various mythos about making deals with fairies and devils and many otherworldly beings. There was truth in these legends. These were the cash and currency of the Kin. As the most neutral party within any territory, we also got saddled with maintaining their books. It kept everyone honest, at least.

"Gah, I hate having to trade up." I groaned from across the room. Bending over, I opened the small refrigerator by the side of my desk and pulled out a cold bottle of beer. I grabbed a double-caffeinated can of coffee and tossed it toward Malik.

"Heads up."

His eyes darted up from the ledger at the movement, and he reached out to catch the can, then set it down on the table next to him. He nodded in thanks and continued to thumb through the ledger. He stretched his neck and set the book aside. Then closed his amber eyes and pulled his glasses off. Rubbing the bridge of his nose, he continued.

"You could hopscotch it," he offered.

Hopscotching a debt was a term used when you strung a bunch of debts together, in hopes of them falling into place like dominoes. Maybe I wanted tickets to a Knights Game. I know that Tsien Tang owns the Knights and can get me the tickets, so I ask him. He says sure, but I gotta get him VIP tickets for the magic show at the Fountains, which has been sold out for 6 months. Ok. So I know who holds Season VIP tickets and doesn't always use them. I go to Eberly and see if she's willing to release her tickets for the show. Sure, but she wants in on a high-stakes private game being held by Vincencio De La Cruz. And so on.

Malik was suggesting I tap one of the other Kin for their debt over Tatiyana and see what they would want in trade for it.

Because Tatiyana sure as shit wasn't willing to deal.

I popped the cap off of my bottle and flopped down into the high-backed ergonomic chair behind the desk. Its springs squeaked a little.

"Hey, take it easy. That's a three-grand chair." Malik frowned at me.

I glanced at him over the top of my bottle, leaned back, and propped my feet up on the carved cherry wood desk that I had inherited from August Murr.

Malik's eyes widened. "That is a made-to-order bespoke, Scully & Scully leather-topped partner's desk. You have no shame." He shook his head.

"Nope," I replied and took a long drag off of the bottle. "OK. So... IF... and I mean IF... we try to hopscotch this, who do we have that has the debt we need?"

Malik continued to stare at my feet on the all-too-expensive piece of furniture. I rolled my eyes and sighed, then threw my legs back down. "Fine."

"Thank you." He returned to glancing through the ledger.

"How do you feel about Tsien Tang?" Malik asked. I choked on my beer.

"I like him just fine. I like him better when he stays in Spring Valley." I wiped my lips and leaned forward on the desk. A coaster slid across its surface and stopped in front of me. I stared at it.

"If not for the desk, then for me. Please," Malik asked.

I chuckled and set my bottle on the coaster, saving the desk's surface from the wet of my bottle.

"Passing on the dragon. Got it." Malik smiled.

"I'm not looking to enact the nuclear option here, Malik. We just need to find someone who can pull the favor to get her to turn the child over to Oberon, so the Fae-Kin don't end up in an all-out war in the streets."

A shadow crossed my threshold. A figure cut from the stuff of dreams and nightmares. Tall and broad-shouldered, his long russet hair was tied at the nape of his neck and trailed down his back in thick curls. Sparkling green eyes, flecked with gold, smiled at me from across the room. Not everyone can pull off a double-breasted bottle-green herringbone suit. It helps when it's Armani. It also helps when you are Robert Goode.

"I heard you had a problem with my father's ex?"

Goodfellow

"Well, that's my cue to leave." Malik snapped the ledger shut and stood abruptly.

Robert's golden-green eyes followed the other man's movement the way a cat follows prey. He stood tall and stepped out of the doorframe to allow Malik to pass. Malik looked over his shoulder at me.

"Call me when you're ready to work on this. I'll be down at No Quarters." His amber eyes slid over to Robert. "You know, for a man whose entire people pride themselves on their adherence to their word, you are wonting, sir."

Robert blinked, recoiling as if struck.

Malik stepped past him and out the door.

I sat at my desk and watched the exchange, quietly drinking my beer. Robert looked at me, confusion replacing the predatory glint in his eyes.

"You stood him up," I said with a shrug.

Robert's ginger brows knit together. "No, I didn't. The hockey game is Saturday," he countered.

I shook my head. "The Comic Book thing. The graders were gonna be there. You said...,"

Robert's eyes widened. "I would cover the books Malik wanted graded... I thought it was next week. Oh, no." He looked after Malik quickly, searching for the other man. His shoulders sunk.

"I am an asshole." Suddenly, the self-assured air of confidence that he wore a moment ago fell away to nothing.

"Mmmm." I hummed over the rim of my bottle and nodded. "So I have been told."

Robert nodded to himself as if listening to a voice that only he could hear. "Yes, I will have to make it up to him." He paused again and looked over at me with a sheepish blush that colored his entire face and ran down his neck.

"This is not how I had planned to impress you today," he offered.

I blinked and set my bottle on the desk. I paused and reached for the coaster and set the bottle carefully on its absorbent surface. Meeting the eyes of the handsome Fae-Kin that stood across the room from me, I tented my fingers and rested my wrists on the desk's surface.

"The room is yours. Show me what you got."

Robert's left eyebrow twitched up slightly. A grin tugged at the corner of his full lips. He moved to the door and pushed it closed with a single fluid motion and a dancer's grace. It swung free and latched with a solid *click*.

"I love it when you leave options open like that," he replied with a deep rumble in his voice. He reached a broad and well-manicured hand to his throat and tugged at the silk tie knotted there.

I remained in my expensive chair, behind my expensive desk, and let my eyes take in the show before me. While immune to the supernatural charms and magics of the Fae-Kin, Robert Goode was a handsome man with an almost intoxicating natural charisma and charm. Something he no doubt inherited from his father, Oberon Elegast.

He paused in his motions, a moment of darkness passing behind his eyes. "Did she hurt you?" he asked softly.

I shook my head and realized that he would eventually discover the truth of it, regardless. Should I tell him the truth now, or lie and explain later? I shrugged in response. "I have a lovely new Lichtenberg figure up my leg. I may have Savage put ink on it at some point. I'm sure he'd love the challenge."

Robert's jaw tightened and his eyes darkened. His voice dropped. "She could have killed you." Three broad steps brought him across the room to the edge of the desk. He stood in front of me, looking down at my seated figure.

"Tam..."

I shook my head. "It comes with the job, Beto. You know that."

He looked at his hands, then me again. "Doesn't mean I have to like it."

I chuckled and relaxed back into my chair, allowing myself to unwind. Fae-Kin were a capricious group on the best of days. Robert was Oberon's oldest son, and heir apparent. He could just as easily have been here to exact a demand, as ask me to dinner. Part of me found the mercurial moods fascinating. Most of the time, I wanted to shake him.

Sensing my change in mood, he smiled once more, his eyes lighting up with some hint of mischief. He stepped to the corner of the desk, fingers trailing along its ornately carved edge. "You are... well, then?" he asked.

I observed him and slowly pushed the chair back and away from the desk.

"Malik is a very thorough and competent mender," I replied.

Beto's lips pursed together and the corners of his eyes narrowed slightly as he contemplated... something. He rounded the corner of the desk, fingers still dancing lightly across the dark wood. His index finger tapped absently as he regarded me.

The dreams that had helped to fashion the figure of Robert Goode had ridden the coattails of professional magicians and the sparkling headdresses of showgirls. Magic, passion, promises, and broken dreams called to the Fae-Kin. Las Vegas was filled with these. It was no surprise that their people occupied a large population in the City of Second Chances. How many came to the City for riches, only to find themselves broken and destitute? The City was the fabled pot of gold at the end of the rainbow made real.

Or at least there was enough of that belief present for the Fae-Kin Courts to call home.

Every Kin had a specific method of creation. The Blood and Shifter Kin required an exchange of blood and the recipient surviving the resulting infection. Spirit-Kin opened themselves to being inhabited by otherworldly beings. Fae-Kin were crafted from the dreams of mortals that were then infused into a living human body. This infusion resulted in a new Fae-Kin being created. A Changeling child that would take the place of the original human. Once upon a time, Fae-Kin would steal children from mortals to enact this process and increase their ranks. Some still observed this practice. Mortals knowing about the Kin might offer children to the Courts in exchange for favors.

Robert Goode had been a tithe to Oberon countless centuries past. A mortal woman had given herself to Oberon and promised the Fae Laird the resulting child. He had worn many names over the centuries. Old Hob. Pwca. Phouka. Robin Goodfellow. Puck.

Strong, manicured fingers wrapped around my forearm and gently, but firmly, pulled me from my chair and into his arms. I looked into the eyes of the Fae-Kin Heir. A fine layer of russet stubble graced his broad jaw and chin.

"We can't do this," I whispered.

He leaned down, his lips grazed my ear. I heard his deep voice purr, "Previous experience tells me otherwise." There was the smell of whiskey on his breath. My hands slid up his chest as I moved against his firm form. He pushed us both gently forward. The edge of the desk pressed against the back of my thighs. His tongue gently tasted the skin along my neck. I shivered.

"Beto... you know what happens when we do this," I breathed. He was warm against me.

Beto's lips left my neck and found my ear once again. "We end up exhausted and happy for a couple of hours?" he asked.

He wasn't wrong.

Bruce Wayne is a Whore

Dating Robert Goode was not a smart move on my part.

"Shows favoritism," Dean had cautioned me when I had first taken on the Vegas Shard.

I'm sure it did, but the alternatives were not terribly appealing. I could live my life alone and not get involved with anyone. I could get involved with a regular person and risk the Kin manipulating them to get to me. Or I could take a lover from the ranks of the various paranormal entities that I was now aware of.

It was like being a superhero in one of Malik's comic books. I suddenly understood why Bruce Wayne was always such a whore. And I hated it.

I stepped out of the ensuite bathroom that was attached to my office, toweling off my hair. Beto was sitting behind my desk, leaning back in my far-too-expensive chair, his feet propped up on desk's surface. I was reminded of Malik's outburst earlier. At least his shoes were off.

He lolled his head in my direction and smiled warmly.

"She walks in beauty like the night..." he began.

I rolled my eyes at the comment and walked back over to where my abandoned and half drunk bottle of beer sat. It had been moved to a side table earlier. I grabbed it and took a long pull from its dark contents.

"I think we can jump past the poetry part, Beto."

He shrugged and kicked his feet off of the desk, swiveling around and standing in a graceful motion.

"As you wish," he smiled.

"Not that I am not glad to see you, but..."

"Did I stop by on my own, or on my father's bidding?" he finished. He glanced around the office, searching for something. "Ah!" he exclaimed, and bent over to pick up his tie from the floor. He smoothed it out and draped it around his neck. "Little of column A, little of column B," he admitted.

I sighed and shook my head. "Alright, what does he want?" I asked.

"Besides the child that Anya has unlawfully stolen from him?" he said, referring to Tatiyana.

I shrugged. "To be determined on that, but yes."

"Fair," he agreed. He buttoned his shirt front to the collar and looped his tie into an intricate knot. "He wants it settled by MidSummer."

I choked on the liquid in my mouth. "Excuse me?" I sputtered. It was already just past Father's Day. Mid-Summer was less than two weeks away. "There are mundane legal matters involved in this! I don't control the fucking legal system, Beto!" I shouted at him.

"I know." He fastened his French cuffs neatly.

"Your father's an asshole," I muttered.

"Mmm. I know." He nodded and reached for his jacket,sliding it on expertly and tugging at the hem. His green-gold eyes smiled at me as he stepped across the room. He gathered me into his arms and looked down at me. "You, my dear Tamara Lyn Hunter, are beautiful, stalwart, and wise." He pressed his lips to my forehead as I bristled at the situation. "And in no way would I negatively impact my father's interests by telling you that Ambroginio might be able to help you." He murmured against my flesh.

The name sat heavy in my ears.

The City of Las Vegas was incorporated in 1905. Its oldest inhabitants were Shifter-Kin and Fae-Kin, followed by Spirit-Kin. The Blood-Kin had not come to Vegas until the late 1970s and early 1980s. The increase in paranormal romance movies and novels during those decades, the dreams and desires of mankind, began to manifest a place where the Blood-Kin could find a comfortable home. Largely confined to cities in the old world, or enclaves of superstition until then, the Blood-Kin did not reach a height of power on the West Coast of the United States until the latter part of the previous century.

Ambroginio D'Angelo was a recent arrival in the City. Recent being a relative term. He was Blood-Kin, ancient, and often bored. Not always a great combination of traits.

"I... see," I replied carefully.

Beto pulled back and looked down into my eyes. His left hand gently cupped my cheek as his thumb stroked my cheekbone. "I have to go make things better with Malik. Maybe we can have dinner later?" His deep voice rumbled in his chest.

The touch of his fingers on my skin was like fire and electricity all at once, warm and stimulating, and it had nothing to do with magic. "Provided Ambroginio doesn't eat me," I replied, even as I leaned into his touch.

Robert chuckled deeply. "That would be one way for him to meet his ultimate death." He leaned down and placed his lips gently on mine. Whiskey and blackberries. He pulled back, smiled, and winked. "See you later," he purred, then turned to leave, bending to scoop his shoes up. Hooking them over two fingers, he carried them out as he left my office, a lilting whistle on his lips.

Dammit.

Dean had left quite a few things out of what I could expect as a Shard Keeper. I mean, sure, he told me a lot about what was expected of me, but personal things like limitations on romantic partners and having to be responsible for a bunch of entities far older than I was? Ya, he missed those key details.

In his defense, I suppose there is really no good way to tell someone, "Hey, the spirit of the City has decided it wants to make a permanent home with you. You good with that?" If I stop to think about it, I suppose it was like some kind of cosmic matchmaking service. The difference being I didn't remember signing up for it.

It had been a late autumn evening. The heat from the strip was sweltering. People came in to the cafe off of the street just to get a breath of cool air. We'd closed up shop early that night. Dean said there was something he wanted to talk to me about. I thought I was getting canned. I could not have been further from the truth. You remember all those movies where the normie finds out that the world around them is filled with supernatural creatures and they are some chosen one, destined for some weird prophecy? You remember their responses? Ya, it had gone a little like that.

"It happens sometimes," Dean shrugged and offered me a drink.

I snatched it from his hand and gulped it down swiftly. "You say that so easily."

He nodded and refilled my glass. "Most of the time, we can predict which way the City is going to go, and narrow candidates down much earlier," he offered.

"Wait, you mean this isn't a done deal? I may not have to do this?" I wiped the back of my hand across my mouth and paused, staring at Dean. One cat, a ginger tom, meowed suddenly and hopped up onto our table. He shoved his head into my hand and purred loudly. I closed my eyes and scratched his ears out of habit.

"There are others, yes," Dean replied. He took a breath and rubbed the back of his neck. "I was honestly hoping that you'd get recruited for my team, Lyn. I never thought the Shard would pick you as a host."

Suddenly, I was a little insulted.

"Why, because I'm a woman?" I demanded.

Dean blinked and held up his hands. "No. Not at all."

"Because I don't come from some prestigious lineage? That's how this shit plays out in the books, right?"

Chili, the tom, burrowed his face deeper into my hands and purred louder, as if in response to my upset. Dean watched the cat and set his glass down.

"The City wants what it wants, Lyn."

"But you don't approve."

"That is not what I said at all," Dean countered. "A Shard can wear whatever face it thinks best suits it."

"August Murr didn't approve."

Dean shrugged again. "Auggie is from a different time and embodied a distinct set of ideals. Time marches on, and... August Murr is not the cut of suit that the Shard wants to wear any longer."

"What if I say no?" I asked.

The question hung in the air like a great stinky balloon. Outside the cafe, people walked back and forth, laughing, talking on their phones. The neon lights of the City flashing all around them, as they passed by completely unaware of the conversation that was taking place twenty feet away from them.

Chili meowed loudly and sat. He reached out and pawed gently at my hand, tapping it softly with his creamsicle colored foot.

"Then... you say no," Dean replied.

"Just like that?"

"Just like that." He waved at the bottle once more. "No catches. No tricks. It doesn't work if you aren't willing."

I nodded, and he filled my glass once more. Chili tapped at my hand again, asking for attention. I began to pet him once again. He flumped down on the table and leaned against me.

"And I don't end up dead in an alleyway, or in a coma in some hospital?" I asked.

Dean shook his head. "No reason. Doubtful most folks would believe you, and those that would are probably already in the know."

"Ok, that's some bestselling fantasy level bullshit, Dean."

He shrugged. "It's just how it all works. You're a Candidate. It means you get to keep your memories... if you want to."

I nodded in thanks as he topped off my glass once again and lifted it to my lips. "So, how come you remember all of this? Are you one of them?"

Dean smiled a little at that. He looked down at his own glass and swirled it around gently. He watched the ice cubes as they circled the dark liquid, memories playing behind his eyes. He looked up at me, ice-blue eyes meeting warm brown. They were almost sad.

"I said no."

No Quarters

Lights flashed and blinked as a chorus of electronic sounds flooded the air. This was not a casino, though the sounds, lights and loss of money might equate to the same experience for many. Servers wore red t-shirts with the word "NERD" proudly stamped in white ink across the chest. They deftly maneuvered through the sea of bodies that occupied various video arcade games. A few tables and booths were scattered along the walls where patrons sat sipping beverages and eating their favorite game fare.

No Quarters was located a block away from the Convention Center in what used to be a shipping and receiving company building. The company had gone under a couple of years back, and an investor opted to take over the building. The open floor plan of the warehouse proved to very easy to transition into a gaming center. It was within quick walking distance of the monorail, which provided easy access to the arcade, the Convention Center, and many of the larger and more frequently visited attractions along the strip. Like almost everything else in this part of the city, No Quarters was open 24 hours a day.

I had waited thirty minutes before calling down to the store to see if Malik was still there. The owner was a Shifter-Kin named Kenny Yazzi. Kenny and Malik had known each other for as long as either of them was willing to admit. If I ever needed to find Malik, I knew Kenny would be there to help.

I leaned on the bar's surface and nodded to Kenny. He smiled a wide and toothy grin and sauntered over to meet me.

"How is the City tonight, Hunter?" he asked.

"Hot, crowded, and under a deadline."

"Ya?" he nodded in thought. "That have anything to do with why Goode was in here bothering Malik?"

I shook my head. It was loud in here tonight. "No, that's a separate issue between the two of them."

He nodded again, watching me and smiling. It was a smile that left his lips but never quite reached his eyes.

"You know, if Stratford is bothering you, we would be happy to remind him of his place in things," Kenny said, referring to Robert by calling him after an English city. His family's court originated in the Stratford area of Great Britain centuries earlier.

"There IS a problem with the Stratfords," I began.

"Oh?" Kenny's eyes lit up with interest. He was clearly eager to help.

"Ya. But it has nothing to do with Robert." I reached out and tapped the counter. "Thanks for the offer, Kenny. I'll keep it in mind."

"Ma'ii remembers, Hunter!" he called out after me as I walked away.

Ya, I know.

Some random song from this week's most current pop-star headliner came over the speakers. It mixed with the bells, whistles, auto-tuned vocals, and combat noises from the games. I kept telling myself that next time I would wear ear plugs. Every time "next time" rolled around, I still had none. Kenny could probably make a killing labeling ear plugs as a prize for the ticket games.

I shook my head, trying to clear it. So many distractions.

Malik stood at a large pinball machine along the far wall of the floor. I wove my way through the players and approached the game. The chrome and neon lights of the game shone and glittered brightly. Glow-in-the-dark, illuminated painted patterns under black lights depicted a group of adventurers battling a mythological monster. A polished chrome ball shot up the side rail and through the ball gate, depressing the roller wire, and entering play. Robert was nowhere to be seen. I really hoped they had mended their fences.

Malik's eyes were focused on the game. They twitched slightly in my direction as I stepped up to the side of the machine. His fingers tapped the flipper buttons quickly, double bouncing the ball back into play and toward one target. An abandoned glass with half melted ice and condensation coated sides sat at the table next to him.

"Well, that didn't take long. Robbie must be losing his touch," Malik commented without looking over at me.

It was going to be one of those conversations. Ok.

"Why you gotta be like that about him?"

Malik pursed his lips and shrugged as he shifted his weight slightly and leaned in to the machine while tapping the buttons again. His eyes danced from the play space to the display screen where the word "TILT" was painted on the glass. It was dark. He continued.

"I dunno, because it goes against everything you are supposed to represent?" he commented. "You know, neutrality, keeping everyone from tearing each other and the City to pieces and leaving a desolate husk in the middle of the Nevada desert?" His middle fingers tapped as he leaned in with the palms of his hands against the corners of the machine. The ball flew up and into play once more. It bounced off of two bumpers before being drawn into the well where it sat for a heartbeat before it was thrown out and back into play. "Or have you forgotten that part?"

I wanted to punch him for his words. He was right, so I didn't.

"I won't let that happen," was all I could say.

Malik shook his head and continued to play his game. He leaned in once again, hands pressing and massaging plastic and metal with expert skill. Suddenly bright red lights came up on the glass screen and the familiar "Wup-wup-whooooo" tone that accompanied failure sounded. The word "Tilt" flashed as the machine froze and the chrome ball ceased bouncing, falling toward the center of the game.

Malik swore, slammed the glass, and turned to me.

"I really hope not, Tam." His eyes met mine. They were filled with an age and knowledge far beyond his figure. "I can't imagine the devastation if you did." He reached up and rubbed his face with his right hand, smoothing at a beard that was not there. He'd been clean shaven as long as I had known him, but that was a learned gesture.

"What are our options?" He asked, suddenly abandoning the topic and shifting it to something more professional.

Ok, we can practice avoidance. For now.

"What do we have on Ambroginio D'Angelo?" I asked.

Malik's eyes widened slightly, and he nodded in thought. His hand once more smoothing at whiskers that no longer occupied his face. He pinched his lower lip between his thumb and forefinger.

"That might work. Let's hit the Library."

I looked over at the glass on the table and nodded toward it. "You gonna finish that?"

Malik scoffed. "No, thank you. That's an attempted peace offering from Robbie. I accept it, then I accept his apology. Fae-Kin contractual obligations and such. He can stew." He raised his hand and waved at Kenny. The Shifter-Kin nodded and waved back at him across the room.

It was going to be a long night.

The words on the window used to read "Las Vegas City Museum". Below, smaller words said, "Open by appointment only." It avoided the obvious false front of an antique bookstore, or an occult shop at least. Old paintings and pictures from the founding of the City lined the walls. Drawings and sculptures from artists no one remembered were on display in the building's front.

Pictures of several persons, who had been high-dollar investors in the City's foundation, covered one wall.

Cobwebs and dust covered everything that could be seen from the sidewalk. Faded paint that was partially scraped off labeled the windows. It looked like an abandoned odds and ends shop. Cursory observation from anyone passing by leant to the impression that this was a shop that had fallen on hard times, but the owners were still hanging on to it.

The truth of the matter was something very different.

The front of the building was exactly as described. A collection of artifacts from various founders and founding families. There was a significant investment in historical accuracy and recording here if one took the time to look things over. An old cash register and glass case occupied one side of the room. A door led to a back room where a very typical looking desk and computer sat. A narrow bookcase held a selection of reading materials. Some current, some older. It was a comfortable office, if nothing else.

Installing a door behind a hidden bookcase was really not that hard. You would walk down to the local hardware store and buy a kit for building it. Installing a latch, pressure plate, and security for it? Not as out of the ordinary as one would think. But why would anyone go looking for a stairway that led to a basement beneath this section of the block? Especially when it didn't exist on any blueprints still in public records?

Malik spent most of his time in the Library. Reading and refreshing his memory on the various occupants of the City, reviewing documents, tracking histories, or just enjoying space away from everything and everyone else above ground. It was a place of protected information that everyone respected.

Over the centuries there had been various attempts at destroying City Libraries. Some or another Kin would get it into their minds that if they destroyed the records, then they would destroy the debts attached to them. Of course, it didn't work like that. Everyone kept their own copies of their individual records, and those records could be recreated ... with effort. There were rumours that Cosimo de Medici ensured that the tradition of bookkeeping for Cities was created in this fashion. Of course, the de Medicis were renowned for their... questionable... banking habits and bookkeeping in the mortal world, so how much of that was the truth I could only guess.

Malik had upgraded some records to electronic format over the last few years. He made certain they were held on servers that did not connect to the outside world. No internet connection. No Wi-Fi. No access to the files except through this location. Air-gapping is what he called it. I nodded and smiled and just let him handle the electronics.

So there we were, sitting in an underground bunker of knowledge, beneath an abandoned storefront that was made up to look like a defunct historical museum.

At least it was comfortable.

"Ambroginio D'Angelo," Malik began. "Estimated age, five hundred years, place of origin, either in Italy or Greece... depending on your sources."

I groaned, "Why?"

Malik shrugged. "Because ancient things like covering their tracks to hide their places of origin?" He looked over at the book sitting next to him on the desk and flipped through a few pages, then turned to his computer screen. The sound of clicking keys filled the air.

"He wouldn't be the first one to capitalize on modern romantic interest in his people. I mean, someone dreamed him up originally... but... he has debts recorded for at least 500 years on the ledger he handed over for transcription and verification when he came here 10 years ago."

"Ok, so why did a five hundred-year-old Blood-Kin up and move to the middle of the Nevada desert?" I asked from the chair I was straddling across from Malik.

More clicking sounds. Then silence. Malik whistled low. "Looks like he came over with the investors of La Piazza."

I frowned. La Piazza had been a sore subject for the City for over a decade. The area in question once hosted one of the oldest casinos on the strip. A series of poor business deals and the recession left it still abandoned. It was prime real estate, vacant, blighted and dying.

"So I am clear, Malik." I leaned back and braced my arms on the back of the chair. "Are you telling me that blighted scab on my City's skin is Ambroginio's fault?" There was a chill in the pit of my stomach.

Malik paused and considered before replying. He steepled his fingers over his keyboard and glanced in my direction. "Fault and blame for something like this is difficult to determine, Tam..."

"But he's involved."

Malik pursed his lips and considered. "It would appear so."

Beto, how did you know about this?

"Alright then." I pushed myself up and out of the chair. "What's the appropriate gift for visiting an ancient hoary fiend of the night?"

Malik blew out loudly. "Uh... victims to sate his hunger come immediately to mind, but we are fresh out of those... thankfully."

I stretched and pondered our options. My eyes caught the glint of light off of a glass frame. An artist's rendering of how the Strip had been envisioned some 70 years earlier. Beneath that was a small sketch on brown butcher paper. Something that had been quickly drafted as a concept for one of the oldest icons in the City.

The Dunes.

"Ambroginio likes architecture, doesn't he?"

Plazma

Blood-Kin were an odd lot. I suppose in retrospect most Kin were odd by definition, but Blood-Kin certainly topped the charts.

All Kin originally came into being because some human, somewhere, believed in the concept of them strongly enough that they were brought into being. Now, this really isn't an odd concept if you stop to think about it. How many stories exist in different legends and mythologies about believing in something strongly enough, that you can manifest it? This just happened to be a truism that most people didn't realize was... well... true.

Blood-Kin, more commonly referred to as Vampires, had existed throughout mankind's history for as long as anyone could remember. The Greeks had legends about them dating back thousands of years. Shadowy, ephemeral creatures that hovered around the edges of the land of the dead. The only way they could communicate with the real world was to be fed blood. We have Homer to thank for those.

Everywhere there was death or misfortune, there was Blood-Kin. They were there for the creation of loss, fear, anger, jealousy and desire. Women who lost children blamed Aswang or Pennangalan. That same fear and belief made those Blood-Kin real. Husbands who were unfaithful to their wives accused their liaisons of being supernatural creatures, sent to lure them away. Those lies breathed life into the same creatures.

The downside was that once a Kin was created, they often wreaked havoc on the humanity that birthed them. Sometimes they would live in harmony, but those cases were few and far between. They could be bane or boon, depending on what formed them. Most of the time, emotions and dreams strong enough to bring a Blood-Kin into existence meant that the creation was NOT benevolent. They might be able to change that with time, but most embraced their calling with passion and dedication.

The Dark Ages and the Inquisition birthed a whole cadre of Old World Blood-Kin that relished in the role that had been created for them. Unfortunately, their uncontrolled blood carnage also made them easy targets for mortals. Scared humans are dangerous humans. Scared humans also tended to destroy anything they didn't understand, including City Shards. How many times did we lose London and Constantinople? How close were we to the total annihilation of both of those areas of civilization? Clever hands managed to save both of those Shards. The combined councils of the City Kin placed a tight rein on the Blood-Kin after those missteps. Their actions affected the whole of the City, and they had to be more careful, or everyone would end up dead.

But that was just Europe.

Nowadays, many Blood-Kin wanted nothing to do with the roles that history had assigned to them. They were no longer creatures solely confined to the shadows of nightmare. They were alluring, tempting, and powerful. Modern media had given them the option of being something other than the terrifying monster in the shadows, and some of them relished that opportunity. Others still cleaved to the role that had been assigned to them. I'm sure there was a whole civil war going on where that was concerned. But it was not my problem tonight.

My problem involved the Fae Courts of Las Vegas and the ownership of a child.

A large section of humanity knew about the presence of Kin within their ranks. Kin were the creations of humankind, after-all. Embracing their existence just made sense. Trying to keep the supernatural secret from the eyes of mortal man was reserved for poorly conceptualized tabletop games and awful movies. Nonetheless, the majority of humanity were blissfully unaware that the person riding the bus next to them was a Shifter-Kin on their way to a job interview in downtown, or the barista that made the super cool designs in the foam of their latte every morning was Fae-Kin. One merely needed to look at the crap that happened every day to realize that most of humanity was more than happy to bury their heads in the sand and ignore what did not affect them directly. It made the business of Kin easier, certainly.

No matter the role they had chosen to take on, one thing bound Blood-Kin together - a need to sustain themselves on life's essence. Dead bodies ended up in the morgue on a daily basis in every City. It was common. But a sudden influx of corpses missing their requisite eight to ten units of blood? That drew attention that no one wanted. Kin who relied on less-than-savory-sustenance were very careful in the modern era, to ensure their meals were obtained without the mass slaughter of the Middle Ages.

Flashing neon and loud music. It was the standard for downtown Vegas. I kept hoping that one night I might walk into a club that was less cheap glitter and more art museum. I was clearly in the wrong city for that to happen.

A hot pink and turquoise neon sign displayed a bottle dripping single droplets into a glass. With each pink droplet, a letter appeared that spelled the name out.

Plazma.

It was an overdone trope, but it was a trope for a reason, I suppose.

I looked over at Malik. "Seriously?"

Malik shrugged.

A line of patrons waiting to enter the club ran down the sidewalk. They stood against the painted black wall of the club, behind a velvet rope designed to keep order. There seemed no rhyme or reason to their choice of attire. Some were dressed in suits and ties, others in gothic Lolita cosplay, others were decked out in leather and masks. It was quite the assortment.

A man dressed in a tuxedo and looking very much like a maitre'd stood at the door. His long raven black hair was pulled back and tied into a topknot. An athletic-looking woman in a burgundy suit stood behind him. Her hair was close cropped and I could see she had an ear bud in her right ear.

So she's the muscle. Got it.

The host turned hazel-green eyes in my direction, looked me up and down, and smiled a smile that was clearly practiced.

"Do you have a reservation?" He asked.

Malik reached into the breast pocket of his light-weight jacket and pulled out a slim silver card with no markings on it.

"Shard Hunter. She doesn't need one." He smiled back, meeting the host's gaze with his own.

The host's right eyebrow twitched almost impercep-tibly. The practiced mask broke for a space of a heartbeat as he turned to look at me with renewed interest. The woman behind him looked me up and down, clearly sizing me up.

"Librarian Shah. On business tonight, I see," the host replied.

"Are you going to let us in, Yannis, or are we going to stand here comparing... pleasantries...?" Malik asked as he slid the card back into his dark blue jacket.

"Here to see anyone specifically?" Yannis asked, look-ing at Malik. He licked his lips.

I reached up and snapped my fingers in front of Yan-nis' perfect eyes. "Over here, pretty boy. Ya. Ambroginio D'Angelo."

Yannis blinked and snapped his attention back in my direction. He pursed his lips into a fine line. "Shard's got spice this time, I see."

"Shard's on a timeline, and got shit to do. Are we done?"

The woman behind Yannis grinned a little at the comment. "I'll take 'em in, Yani." Her voice was smooth and warm, like rum.

Yannis harrumphed in my direction and turned his attention back to the line.

The woman gestured widely that we should proceed with her and then touched her ear piece. "Potential 916. Repeat 9-1-6". She whispered and then escorted us inside.

I'm not sure what I was expecting when we walked through that dark doorway and into the Club. Maybe I had read too many paranormal romance books growing up, or watched too many bad dramas on late-night TV. I think I had visions of a dark, and all too loud dance club, with dozens of people packed on a dance floor, all writhing to industrial goth music.

That is decidedly not what I saw.

Sure, there was a dance floor, but there were maybe a dozen couples on it, all clearly focused on each other. The lights were dim, but they seemed to be promoting a sense of intimacy over anonymity. There was music, someone was in a sound booth manning the feed. They looked like a college kid, but were geared up with enough tech to have walked out of some dystopian cyber novel.

There was a lot of money involved there. That was an investment.

Around the dance floor were private booths set up into alcoves. Each alcove was adorned with heavy velvet curtains. Some of the alcoves had their curtains drawn closed. Others were open. Each alcove was furnished with comfortable seating, maybe a pair of chairs, maybe a chaise lounge, and a table.

People occupied the alcoves, engaged in conversation.

The strange assortment of guests outside the club was repeated inside as well. One alcove was occupied by a gentleman in a finely tailored gray suit and a pair of young women wearing cat ears. He was serving them what appeared to be tea.

In another alcove, a woman in a high-necked black ball gown reclined on a purple velvet chaise. Seated at her feet was another woman, reading aloud to her from a book. I couldn't catch the title.

I leaned over to Malik. "Fetish club?" I asked.

Malik shrugged a little. "Sort of?" he replied.

The woman who was our escort caught my question. She chuckled a little. "Sounds like Dean left some gaps in her training, Shah."

"I'm working on it, El," he answered.

Across the room, someone pushed what looked like a butler cart toward one of the alcoves. It was skirted in dark black fabric. The person pushing it was dressed in black scrubs. The top of the cart was covered in medical supplies. The overhead lights glinted off of the stainless of the instruments. They paused at an alcove and knocked politely on the frame of the entrance. The pair within, both of them men, looked up at the sound. They looked at one another. One of them nodded. The other gestured for the attendant to enter. The butler cart was pushed inside the alcove and the attendant drew the curtain closed behind them.

Realization dawned on me.

Well shit, that's one way to do it. Hell of a lot cleaner than biting someone.

El must have noticed the light bulb going off in my brain. She nodded and commented, "We employ a staff of 20 full-time phlebotomists trained in various blood-letting techniques. All the donors are screened for disease, are of legal age, and every one of them signs a consent form before being added to the donor pool."

"And the... costumes?" I asked.

El frowned a little at my comment. "Different Kin have different nutritional needs, Shard Hunter." Simply put. "Would you rather have two score Blood-Kin prowling your City at night, and hunting humans like wild animals?"

The thought did not sit well with me.

"I see your point."

"We do make every effort to be reasonable," El said. She led us through the labyrinthine club to a set of stairs that led to a balcony that overlooked the dance floor. Eyes followed us as we walked past the various clients and donors. It was clear that we were something of interest, to be watched and followed. El removed a black velvet rope from the stairwell and gestured. "Papous D'Angelo is expecting you."

Of course he was.

Turkish Delight

"You don't have to do it if you don't want to, Tamara," Dean said.

We had been hashing out the details of taking on the City Shard for a couple of hours. We'd already torn through two burgers and an onion bloom from Cali's and were working on finishing our drinks. It was a heavy meal for an old guy like him, but it didn't seem to bother him at all.

"Ya, I know. You've said that like … twelve times … over the last week, Dean. I get it." I was still salty about the whole deal. Dean assured me I could just walk away from it all if I wanted to. But how do you do that once you find out about this stuff?

There's a whole other world interwoven with the one you have been living. The City is really a sentient entity. You can access all of this new information, or you can go back to cleaning up at the Cat Cafe.

Was there really ever a choice?

Dean had said that he had been approached and offered the opportunity once, but he had turned it down. I still could not wrap my head around that.

"So let me get this straight," I said. I look a long pull off of my cola. "It could have been you instead of August Murr?"

Dean shook his head and set his iced tea down. "No. I was not a candidate for Vegas."

I frowned and rubbed the back of my neck. "Ok. So, you aren't from here then?"

Dean shook his head. "Nope. I'm from the Midwest originally." He smiled his award-winning smile.

Of course he was. If anyone seemed to be the walking embodiment of white-bread Americana, it was Dean Franklin. That made sense.

"Ok, Norman Rockwell."

"Rockwell was from New York." Dean corrected me. "I was a Cedar Rapids boy."

I thought about the comment.

"Well, that's ... the middle of ... nowhere."

Dean cocked a slightly graying eyebrow in my direction and sat back. He pulled the napkin from his lap and tossed it on the table. "It's one of the largest cities in the world for corn processing, the headquarters for Quaker oatmeal, there are world class arts and cultural festivals there and it is the home of the world's largest collection of Masonic materials through the Masonic Library and Museum."

"Oh. Well. I apologize. I did not know ..." I held my hands up.

"You did well enough in your history classes, " Dean began, then stopped himself. "Though your focus was more on this area and the Southwest. I shouldn't expect you to know about Cedar."

"You seem very proud of your hometown." I set my cup down on the table. The condensation ran down the side and formed a ring on its surface. "Why'd you say no?"

Dean's eyes lost their sparkle for a moment as the memory of that decision clearly climbed to the surface of his thoughts.

"Same reason most boys that age make poor decisions. There was a girl."

My eyebrows rose into my hairline. I don't know why I found that to be such a weird answer. Dean seemed a perfectly acceptable type of guy that someone his own age would have been happy to have. But the idea of him being young and foolish didn't sit right with me. He always seemed so together.

"You find that unbelievable?" he asked.

"What? No. Of course not. I'm sure you ... totally ... dated when you were my age." This was an awkward conversation to have with someone who was a parental figure.

Dean shrugged and gathered up our trash. "Let's just say that ... Kin in every City try to make sure their preferred candidate gets chosen. And some of them are not above maneuvering other candidates out of the way."

Ouch. Ok. That was a time bomb of a discussion that we would not have tonight. I sat quietly and watched him clean up our table. He finally looked back over at me.

"A conversation for another time?"

"Deal."

We never got to have that conversation. Or a conversation that would have prepared me for what to expect when I walked into Plazma.

Stop a moment and think. No. Really. Stop for a moment and think about it. In your mind, what do you see when you picture a vampire? Something that has existed for centuries, born from dread and fear in a time long before electricity. A time before the printing press... when humans still fully embraced the legends and myths of the ancient world as something real.

Do you have that picture in your mind?

Good.

Now wad it up and throw it out the window.

Plazma was nothing like I thought it would be. Ambroginio D'Angelo was the same.

The upstairs balcony area of Plazma resembled a comfortable office that overlooked the club area. From this vantage, anyone standing at the railing could see every aspect of the club and its attendees. The alcoves were closed off from the floor, but the ceilings were made from one way glass. Those inside the rooms could not see up and out, but whoever was up here could look down and see what was happening inside.

Part of me found that a terrible violation of privacy and wondered if those within the alcoves knew this. Another part of me said this was none of my business and warned me to not get involved. If D'Angelo wanted to play voyeur, that was between him and his patrons.

Seated at an elegantly dressed table was a man. He had the olive-toned skin of the Mediterranean, and thick black hair. A bushy mustache that would have given a 1970s porn star a run for their money occupied his upper lip. He wore a white, low cut tank top that revealed a tan, oiled, and hairy chest. Over that was a short-sleeved linen shirt, worn open. Matching white linen pants accompanied his outfit, and he was positively dripping with gold chains and bangles. A stack of papers sat before him on the table. He casually looked through them, frowning once in a while and setting some papers to the side. His nails were perfectly manicured and his fingers adorned with large gold rings.

As we cleared the threshold, he looked up from the table.

And smiled.

The whole of his face lit up with joy and life at our appearance. It was the smile of a grandfather, happy to see his favorite grandchild. He pushed away from the table and stood, opening his arms wide.

"Welcome to Plazma, Tamara Hunter!" his voice was deep and full. "May the City always find a place of warmth and welcome here!"

Behind us, El nodded simply and then departed back down stairs.

Ambroginio strode across the room to meet us and pulled me into an embrace before I could say "no." He was not a tall man, maybe five feet nine. But I could feel the strength in his muscles beneath his linen shirt. He smelled like black juniper and cedarwood. He pressed his right cheek to mine and then repeated the gesture on the left. His skin felt like sandpaper.

He pulled back and rested his broad hands on my shoulders. The smile on his face reached his chestnut brown eyes.

"I'm so happy to meet you!" He gently squeezed my shoulders and then dropped his hands. His gaze drifted over to Malik. His eyes softened a little. "Librarian, you have been missed."

Malik looked at the ground and cleared his throat, a little uncomfortable. "I have ... uh ... been busy."

The sudden realization that Malik knew Ambroginio dawned on me. I lolled my head over to Malik. The look on my face said more than words would ever convey. Ambroginio watched the exchange between us and chuckled loudly.

"Now, now, Miss Hunter, don't be too upset with him. I'm sure he would have told you eventually." Ambroginio reached over to Malik and draped his arm across his shoulders casually.

"How can I be of service to our City this evening?" He smiled warmly.

I continued to stare at Malik while I responded to Ambroginio. I reached into the inside pocket of my jacket and carefully pulled out the sketch of the Dunes. It was neatly tucked away in a Ziploc bag. "Dean Franklin told me it was appropriate to bring a gift when meeting the head of a Kinship. I hope you like it."

"Frank was an amazing man. The City is worse off for his loss... oh my god, is that the Dunes?!" Ambroginio all but squealed. He dropped his arm from around Malik and reached for the bag. He wiggled his fingers in anticipation and carefully took it from me. He stared at it and then looked back at me. "Oh, he taught you very well, Shard Hunter," Ambroginio breathed.

The Blood-Kin's attention dropped from Malik and became entirely focused on me. He reached his muscular arm over and pulled me to his side, sliding his arm across my shoulders, and walked us over to the table he had been seated at. Scattered across its surface were ... costume designs. He waved at them casually.

"Ignore those. Tina, over at Caesar's, wanted feedback on some new designs. Looking for something ... authentic ... I am tempted to set these on fire and send her the ashes." He moved to pull a chair out for me.

"Please, let's chat. Coffee?" he asked.

I slowly slid into the chair and allowed him to seat me. He gestured for Malik to take a seat, which he did. Ambroginio held up a finger, asking for a moment, and then boldly strode to the balcony railing. He placed his hands on the edge and then yelled loudly.

"What a terrible lack of manners you all have! Is this how we treat our City?! It's no wonder no one respects us. I want a coffee service up here now!" His voice carried the tone of one who was used to being obeyed. He turned around in a single fluid motion and the smile returned.

"Apologies for that. They forget there is a proper way to do things." He brushed off his pants. "I blame Hollywood, honestly." Movement from the right side of the room caught his eyes. He glanced in that direction and gestured with his fingertips for them to enter. "I understand and respect the importance of intellectual creativity... but really ... some things that come out on film are absolute drivel!" He sighed dramatically then looked back at me.

"But you are not here to talk about Bela Lugosi's horrendous portrayal of my people ... are you?" He strode back to the table. As he did so, a black butler cart emerged from the side of the room, pushed by a young woman in black scrubs. The cart carried a copper and enamel Turkish coffee service, with several ceramic demitasse cups which were seated in copper open-weave containers, and a selection of pastries and tiny candies coated in a white substance.

She quietly pushed the cart over to the table and began making the coffee table-side.

Ambroginio retrieved a black napkin from the cart and snapped it open with a flick of his wrist, then offered it to me politely. "The memory of a cup of coffee lasts forty years." Ambroginio said almost ceremonially. "May this memory be a pleasant one."

"Thank you?"

"The Fae-Kin are not the only ones who remember how to treat our City, Miss Hunter." Ambroginio smiled warmly. His comment was not lost on me. He observed the coffee attendant. His eyes fixated on each of her movements. He nodded slightly once or twice. "You don't have a nut allergy, do you?"

I shook my head.

"Excellent. The Librarian from Xativa neglected to advise the Kinship of the City's allergy to pistachios in ..." he thought a moment, "I want to say 1707, but I may be off on the dates ... Poor dear. The City itself was raided, burned and renamed San Felipe, shortly after the Shard fell ill from a poorly received coffee service. We can't have a repeat of that now, can we?" He glanced briefly toward Malik, who sat silently next to me, hands folded neatly on the table before him.

Well, that was clearly something I needed to ask Malik about later.

The ruling hemophage of Las Vegas reached for a pair of hammered copper tongs and a fine bone china dessert plate. "Baklava, Tulumba ... they are like your churros, but soaked in lemon instead of cinnamon ... and, of course, lokma." He carefully placed a sample of each on the plate and graciously placed it before me. "I believe you call them Turkish Delight ... but have no fear. I'll not drag you away through a wardrobe."

"Coffee is an important part of the culture of my people, Miss Hunter. Not the Kin. The people that created me. I would do their memories a disservice if I did not remember my roots by honoring you in this manner. Thank you for indulging an old man in his ways."

As Ambroginio began the intricate ritual of preparing Turkish coffee, the rich aroma filled the air, triggering an unexpected flood of memories. For a moment, I was transported back to my grandmother's tiny kitchen, where she'd perform a similar ceremony on special occasions.

"The memory of a cup of coffee lasts forty years," Ambroginio said, his voice pulling me back to the present.

I nodded, a lump forming in my throat. "My abuela used to say something similar," I said. "She called it 'cafe de olla' - pot coffee. Said it could wake the dead and make them dance."

Ambroginio chuckled slightly at the imagery. "Ah, a family tradition? Do tell, my dear."

I hesitated, suddenly aware of how personal this memory was. But there was a genuine curiosity in Ambroginio's eyes, and I found myself continuing.

"She... she was from Mexico originally. Came to Vegas young, worked as a housekeeper in the casinos." I smiled softly, remembering. "She always said Vegas was a city of dreams, but you had to be careful which dreams you chased."

Sitting at the table, across from a being that was created from the dreams of other, my abuela's words suddenly took on a new meaning.

Did she know?

As Ambroginio carefully poured the coffee into small, ornate cups, I couldn't help but draw parallels between his meticulous process and my grandmother's ritual. The way he held the cezve, the careful pour, the attention to every detail - it was all hauntingly familiar.

"She would have loved this," I murmured, more to myself than to Ambroginio. "All the ceremony, the respect for tradition. She always said we were losing touch with our roots."

Ambroginio nodded sagely. "Roots are important, especially in a city like Vegas. They keep us grounded when everything else is chaos and illusion."

He carefully offered me my cup. It was filled with the dark liquid and carried a rich, full aroma. The top of each cup of liquid was covered in a smooth crema. I was witnessing true artistry.

His words struck a chord. Since becoming Shard Keeper, I'd been so focused on learning about the supernatural world that I'd neglected my heritage. How much of my grandmother's wisdom could apply to my new role? I didn't know her for long, but maybe there was something there I could eventually use.

As Ambroginio handed me my cup, our eyes met. For a moment, I saw past the ancient Kin to the man he must have once been - someone who understood the importance of tradition and memory.

"To roots," I said, raising my cup slightly.

A smile played at the corners of Ambroginio's mouth. "To roots," he agreed. "And to new growth."

Malik was served as well, and then Ambroginio casually dismissed the attendant. He leaned back in his comfortable chair. The countenance that had once been warm and inviting shifted slightly as the predator beneath the glitzy skin surfaced for a moment.

"Now then, pleasantries and formalities aside, you've clearly come to ask me for something. What might that be?"

Trust Issues

"Well, that is a terrible predicament for our City to be in, I agree." Ambroginio pursed his lips and nodded. He lolled his head back and stared at the ceiling in thought. "It's a shame that the Fae-Kin continue to play these terribly droll little games with each other every century. More-so that they continue to involve the innocent." His fingers tapped on the table, the gold and diamonds on his rings sparkling and glinting in the overhead lights.

He looked over at me then. "I'm afraid I can't help you, Miss Hunter. Yes, the Fae going to war in the middle of the Strip will be alarming, to be certain. It would be a terrible thing, if the Laird could not control her vassals.

It might prove her unworthy of her nobility … but you can't expect me to just hand over the debt she owes me, to keep the peace between her and Elegast. Fae debts are pricey things, and they rarely allow themselves to be caught up in one."

"What would you like in exchange?" Malik asked softly.

"So direct, Librarian," Ambroginio chastised.

"Blame me, not him. I'm clearly a bad influence," I interjected. The coffee service had been amazing. Growing up in the foster care homes, I was lucky to have crap grounds run twice through the same filter. This? This was something else.

I had been cautious about accepting food from D'Angelo, but Malik reminded me that my health could directly impact the health of the residents of the City, and therefore the health of the blood that the Kin fed upon. While it would not have been out of the scope of things for Ambroginio or other Kin to poison or influence the health of humans through a food source, I was clearly off-the-menu for such things.

"Hardly," Ambroginio commented. "It's nice to have a woman at the reins. Murr was a bully and, if we are being honest, an asshole." He turned his brown eyes to me. "You are a woman who knows what she wants, and one capable of voicing those needs and desires. Any man would be lucky to have such a partner. It's commendable

... and novel. I like it." He pushed a demitasse spoon around on the tablecloth absently. "But our dear Malik is correct. Something for something is the currency of barter and trade."

"The City could ... see its way clear ... to ... permit you to create one of your own?" I offered carefully.

"Tam!" Malik exclaimed next to me. He knew exactly what I had just offered.

While Kin were initially created from the manifest will of humanity, they each also possessed the ability to self-replicate and increase their ranks from within. It was not a simple task for most of them, and for others, it was damned near impossible. Legends of Vampires creating more of themselves through the transference of ... something ... were not too far off the mark. A Blood-Kin might gift a human with Kinship, but the chances of the transference going horribly wrong were very high. Both Blood-Kin and Shifter-Kin suffered the same malady. Most humans were ill-equipped to become vessels for their Kinship, and the transference usually ended in the recipient's death. Granting Blood-Kin a permit of transference meant allowing them the potential ability to kill multiple humans before the transference finally took.

D'Angelo had created Plazma to reign in the rampant hunting that had occurred in Vegas before his arrival. I was counting on that spark of decency to win out over what I had just offered.

Take a chance and roll the dice.

He regarded me silently from across the table. His perfectly manicured fingers toyed with the edge of the spoon as he studied me. The City Shard that I had bonded with prevented him from using any of his Kin abilities on me, so he could not read my mind, or force my hand through tricks of magic. He was forced to assess me as a normal human might.

A normal human that was five hundred-year-old.

"Very. Tempting." He replied.

Malik sat next to me, shaking his head and staring at the edge of the table. I could tell he was not thrilled with my chances.

Ambroginio tugged absently on the rightmost edge of his mustache in thought. His eyes were on mine as he continued to try to sus out my motivations and meanings.

"I'm afraid not," he finally said.

I blinked in surprise, while internally I was rejoicing. It meant I had judged him correctly.

"Any Kin I created would be bound to the earth of this City, as I am bound to mine ... and since I would very much like to leave this glitter-filled-repository-of-pubescence ... I must ... regretfully... decline." Ambroginio said each word with measured precision. It was almost painful to listen to.

I paused a moment in my thinking, as his words played back again.

... as I am bound to mine...

Ambroginio wasn't from here. He'd come here with a business group some 10 years earlier. He didn't want to be here. He was BOUND to something they brought with them!

I placed my elbows on the table and then steepled my fingers as I looked across the table at the ancient hemophage.

"Let's talk about La Piazza."

"That was a stupid, stupid move, Tam." Malik chided me as we walked down the street. Hundreds of regular normal humans passed us by, fixated on each other, the lights and sounds around them or their phones. How many of them actually knew what happened around them on a daily basis?

"It was a gamble." I shrugged and shoved my hands into the pockets of my jacket. I silently wished that designers would make women's pants with deeper pockets so I could shove them there.

"It was a ridiculous level of risk for the City!" Malik countered. He had not let up since we parted ways with Ambroginio at Plazma. I appreciated his concern, but he was getting on my nerves.

I grit my teeth and looked at my feet as we walked. He continued his haranguing. At some point, I guess I just tuned him out. There is a point where well-meaning concern and council just becomes nagging. We had passed that level three "I can't believes" and two "I have nevers" ago.

"Dean would not ..."

"Dean is not fucking here!" I snapped at him. I could ignore the fisher-wife nagging for a long while, but invoking Dean? That was a line too far. I turned to face Malik. I could feel the flush of the anger in my face and hear my heartbeat pounding in my head. Could I get high blood pressure as a Shard? What would that look like?

"Dean Franklin is dead, Malik! Ok? He's dead and buried, and I'm terribly sorry that he didn't pass on the ... ancient and hidden knowledge ... he was supposed to before it happened." The words were hard and I felt my chest constrict with tension as I voiced them. "I'm sorry you are stuck with the orphan girl from foster care as the City Shard! But maybe ... just maybe ... you trust the Shard's choice and let me do my goddamn job!" I turned away from him and started walking down the street once more. Several people had stopped to watch the exchange. A couple of teenagers had their phones out and were recording the exchange. It would hit the net in a matter of minutes. I'd be trending in an hour.

Because Kin in the City loved their drama.

By morning I'd have a dozen messages asking if I was ok, flowers, offers to host a spa day. While they all silently traded back room comments about how this brief out-burst could benefit them and their position in the city.

Malik stood where he was, slack jawed at my response. "Tamara ..."

"Go home, Malik." I called back over my shoulder. I caught the eye of one kid with their phone. I pointed at them. "I see you, Sheldon King. Don't make bad choic-es." The teen bobbled their phone and quickly put it away.

The press and throng of the city slowly enveloped itself around me, almost instinctively, like a protective bubble of humanity.

I walked in relative peace and silence for several blocks with no company but my own thoughts. Any other woman walking alone down the strip might have expect-ed a bad turn, but I knew no one would bother me. It was both comforting and depressing at the same time.

I caught movement out of the corner of my eye. A car was pacing me. Seriously? They couldn't even wait until morning. I took a breath and pulled my shoulders back and stretched my neck. I did not look at whoever it was.

"You should keep moving, whoever you are," I said in a tone loud enough to carry over the surrounding din.

The passenger side window slowly rolled down on the Audi R8. It was painted flat black. The polished chrome accents shone brightly against its simple surface. It looked like something out of a comic book.

I recognized it immediately.

"I'm afraid I can't do that." Beto's deep voice called from the vehicle, "I owe you dinner."

I stopped walking.

The car stopped pacing me. Beto reached across the sports car's bucket seats to open the passenger-side door.

"Going my way?" He smiled.

Part of me just wanted to spend the night angry and walking the streets, venting that anger. Another part of me realized that all that would accomplish was morning exhaustion, sore muscles and blisters on my feet. The promise of welcome company, warm hands, and comfort won out.

"Fuck it." I swore. "Ya, I guess I am," I replied and climbed into the waiting vehicle.

There was something about the smell and feel of leather seats that was almost enchanting. A proper choice of words, considering the driver.

Robert watched me climb into the car. He waited patiently for me to get settled. Eyes the color of absinth examined me carefully, notes of concern in their golden flecks. I pulled the seat belt across. It clicked into place.

"Anyplace in particular, or you just want me to hit the Beltway for a bit?" He checked the rearview and side mirrors as he pulled out into traffic.

"Just ... wherever," I said. I closed my eyes and leaned my head back against the seat.

"Mmmmm... inviting." He smirked.

The car glided quickly in and out of traffic, weaving between other vehicles effortlessly.

"Problems with Ambroginio?" he asked.

I shook my head. "No. He's willing to trade. I just have to get something for him in exchange."

"Mmm ... playing hopscotch?"

"Little bit."

I could almost feel him pursing his lips and trying to figure out what the old Kin wanted for the debt that would allow Elegast to claim the changeling child from his estranged spouse. I thought about telling him, but that information was valuable. And dangerous.

Ambroginio was earth bound. Like many vampiric legends of ancient days, he was tied to the land that birthed him. Many times that meant they had to sleep in that soil. Clever Kin had figured out that by placing the soil into fired clay bricks, one could construct buildings from one's home soil, and live damned near any-where. All it took was a backhoe, shipping containers, and someone willing to mix the soil into clay bricks or a cement foundation.

There were, of course, a few downsides to that. The first was, one probably had a limited supply of earth that they could dig up and ship out across the world. The second was, in order to move beyond certain territorial limitations associated with the earth, one had to carry a handful of that earth with them. If Ambroginio want-ed to leave Vegas and couldn't, it meant that someone had taken possession of his golden ticket. He was stuck here until he either found that earth sample, extract-ed enough of his home soil from whatever it had been baked into here, or find the keystone that contained it.

Anyone with that information might control Am-broginio.

I was fond of Beto. Maybe too fond, according to Malik. But I couldn't give him Ambroginio's secret. The Kin of the City would never trust me again.

I suddenly realized the rift that would keep me forever separate from them.

"You good?" he asked quietly.

"Can I ask you something and not have you get butt hurt?" I asked.

Robert's eyes slid over to me and then back to the road. "Ooookkk...?"

"Before I said yes to the City, before all your magical woojie wouldn't work on me ... did you ever use it on me?"

Robert pursed his lips and scowled. "Did Ambroginio make an accusation?"

I blew out air in an exasperated sigh.

"No! Jesus! Why does it always have to be an ulterior motive? Why can't I just be asking a question that -I- want an answer to?!" I folded my arms and folded into myself. Maybe I should have just kept walking.

Beside me, Robert took a deep breath. I could tell he was trying to parse out the right thing to say. Fae and their words. Even now, he was gaming the potential pitfalls associated with any answer he might give.

"No," he finally said. He flipped the turn signal on and zipped through traffic.

I glowered at him. "No, I can't ask?"

His eyes looked up into the rearview mirror and then to me, "No, I never tried to glamor you."

The sincerity in his voice washed over me, easing a tension I hadn't even realized I was carrying.

"I'm sorry, Beto I ..."

"Nope, not accepted," he replied quickly. "You were both right and smart to ask. My father is an asshole, as you have mentioned ... often... and I am his son. It would be within profile for me to do so." He changed lanes again, weaving through the cars with the skill of someone whose life relied on being able to dodge obstacles.

I stared out the window and watched the neon lights blur passed us, obscuring the details of the City.

"Can we just drive for a while?" I asked.

"Yup," came the reply. He dropped his hand down to the shifter and changed gears. "Anything for the lady." He offered me a smile and turned his focus back to the surrounding traffic.

Fuck my life.

One Thing Leads to Another

I was in the position I was in because of my own choices. I had to remind myself of that once in a while. It would have been a lot easier to fall into the whole "Chosen One Fated to Carry This Weight Unwillingly" line, but the truth of the matter was, when it all came down to it, I said yes.

I sat in the Cafe after hours, drinking my coffee and listening to Dean. We'd been talking for the better part of an hour already while I scrubbed counter tops and cleaned cat boxes. I needed to put the cats to bed for the evening soon. The last thing I wanted to do was leave these furry little terrorists out overnight to tear things up while everyone was gone.

I leaned on the counter and listened to Dean. Chili jumped up from the floor and padded over to me. He shoved his orange-colored face into my hand, insisting I give him my attention, right MEOW. I scratched his ears.

"Ok, how does all of this work?"

Dean took a deep breath and rubbed the back of his neck. "You mean the candidate selection?"

"Sure, let's start there."

"So ... many times the Shard is taken on by members of founding families ... when it is just getting its bearings. Vegas became an official City in 1905. There are a handful of families in the city that fit that bill. Two names you probably know - Fremont and Clark. They both had family that carried the Shard of the City for a little while back in the day."

I nodded. Ok that made sense. Bill Clark was a railroad baron who had purchased land in the Glitter Gulch and helped expand the area. Clark County was named for him. John Charles "Pathfinder" Fremont had been a cartographer responsible for helping map the western expansion. Both held places of importance in the city's history.

"I didn't think Fremont was here long enough to really count?" I asked.

Dean nodded a little. "He wasn't. Not really. But the fort they built while they came through here became instrumental in the City's foundation."

Chili purred loudly and flumped down on the counter in front of me. All twenty pounds of him.

"And Clark? I thought he was just a railroad tycoon that bought a bunch of land from some guy named Stewart?"

Dean smiled at me from across the room. "You paid attention in class."

"Whatever, old man." I smiled a little around my coffee cup.

"The historic records are confusing, honestly," Dean said. "There were two shards here for a little while … at the beginning. One that represented the Stewarts and their lands and people, and the other that represented Clark and his."

I nodded and continued to pet Chili.

"And the locals … out at Big Springs? They … never had a say in any of this?" I asked.

Dean was silent a moment as he contemplated his response. The Valley had been occupied for thousands of years prior to the railroad and the colonists seeking to expand ever West. Big Springs was the site of a naturally occurring oasis. It had supplied the valley residents fresh water for generations until it couldn't anymore because of the increased population and pumping.

Had there been no shard here until then? I found that difficult to believe.

"I ... umm ... I don't know," he whispered. "The indigenous people were disbanded ..."

"You mean forcibly relocated."

"Tamara."

"No, say it like it was. The colonists came in, displaced the people, probably destroying the local shard, which allowed them to make room for all of this." I stared at Dean, daring him to deny it.

"I don't know if that's what happened."

I nodded. I grabbed my empty paper coffee cup and tossed it into the recycling can. "You don't need to. I know." I shook my head. "Ok, let's do this. The City wants to look at me? I'm all hers."

Dean balked. "Wait, are you sure?" he asked.

I nodded and then reached back to grab a handful of my hair and tied it into a knot at the base of my neck.

"Ya, I am. She wants a chance to see things from another pair of eyes ... and I'm gonna give them to Her." I scooped up Chili from off of the counter. He meowed in complaint as I carried him over to his kennel. "Take me to whoever I need to meet."

Dean watched and nodded and dragged out his phone. "I'll make the call."

When the City wanted to see things through my eyes, I doubt she anticipated being cuddled up with Robert Goode.

Robert's arm draped around my waist. His body pressed protectively against mine in his sleep. I could feel his face buried in my hair and hear his deep breathing. He sounded like a giant cat purring. It was rhythmic and calming. I had a dozen things that needed doing, but for a few moments, I let myself forget them and just be here.

I shouldn't be here. Neither of us should be. But there was something about him. Maybe I wasn't immune to the charm of the Fae-Kin after all. It would be so much easier if that were the case. No, this was something else. Something ... normal.

I remembered when I met Robert Goode. I was still a Candidate, but I didn't even know that yet. The ceremony had not yet taken place. Hell, I'd not even met August Murr yet. I was a year out of High School. I'd just started working at the Cafe. I was just Tamara Hunter then, and he was a hot mess of trouble that screamed "buyer beware." It was a hot summer night at the raceway.

The community service group Dean had signed me up with had been out at Nellis Dunes that afternoon, cleaning up the trails. I was eighteen. I didn't want to spend my summer doing community service.

"Community Service looks good on a resume, Lyn," he had advised when I balked at the idea. He promised it would be a pleasant experience and he would not ask me again. Dean had not steered me wrong yet. I agreed.

The Dunes Rec area was part of The Mint 400 off-road race that was held annually in March. The race had concluded months ago, but the raceway location was a favorite place for people to dump trash. There were a couple of groups that organized to help keep the area clear of trash for race reasons and to preserve the desert. I spent the late afternoon and early evening with the group. I thought they were going to be a bunch of pretentious eco types. Nope. Turned out they were just a bunch of local business owners who wanted to help take care of the City.

Looking back on it now, I can see why Dean did what he did. He was smooth. I gotta give the old man credit.

Now we sat around a bonfire, resting and enjoying the night. The glow of the city set a glittering skyline backdrop against the purple sky, scattered with twinkling stars. One group had brought up some buggies and there was a little night racing going on.

A sandrail that was not part of our group crested the dunes and rolled into camp. It was a twoseater long travel sand rocket by the looks of her. Painted in greens and golds. The driver rolled up, angling the lights to not blind us. His engine roared across the sand.

Two organizers looked at each other and exchanged quiet words. One of them stood and walked over to the driver. The engine died, and he pulled himself out of the roll cage in a single fluid movement. He wore off-road gear, pants and boots. His jacket was dark green leather, accented in neon green and gold. It looked like a motor-cycle jacket. He tugged off his gloves while he listened to the organizer. Then he nodded and pulled off his helmet.

Russet curls framed his face as he shook out his hair. He was covered in road dirt and sweat. The firelight danced in his absinth green eyes.

"I won't be long then." He smiled at the organizer and when he did, I felt my heart stop.

No, no, no, no. You cannot do this tonight. You do not know who this guy is. Just stay where you are. He'll leave soon, and you will never see him again and every-thing will be just fine.

Then he was walking toward me. The firelight silhou-etted his frame. In that moment, he was a figure from fable, outlined in light armor, his unruly hair a halo of amber wheat grass.

"This seat taken?" he asked.

I trailed my fingers across Robert's freckled forearm. The first rays of dawn danced on the amber-colored hair there. Such a distinct contrast to my own. My hair was black and straight, his russet and full of loose curls. My skin was fawn brown, tawny as they used to call it. He was almost porcelain and dotted with tiny brown freckles. There was no acne, no scars, no ink on him. His skin was smooth and perfect. Even the freckles seemed placed with a precision that would accent his otherworldly nature. As only a creature born of dreams and desires could only be.

The high thread count sheets we were wrapped in made a distinct rustling noise as we both shifted in response to one another. Creams, golds, and green filled the room. His bed was a giant gothic-looking thing with carved posts and almost cathedral-like arches. Heavy green velvet drapes accented it. The wood was dark and rubbed smooth in some areas from what I imagined were centuries of use.

I did not know how old this piece of furniture was, but it was well cared for, and possibly as old as the man who slept next to me.

He's ancient, I reminded myself. When we think of supernaturals, society always assigned the traits of immortality to Vampires and their ilk. But agelessness was not theirs alone. Fae and Spirit-Kin also experienced extended lifespans. Shifters and most Hex-Kin lived typical human life-spans. There were, of course, exceptions.

Malik was one of them.

The Librarian of the City was a Hex-Kin of undetermined age, whose soul was bound to magics not even the Fae could understand.

And he was likely sitting in the Library right now, stewing about our exchange the night before.

Beto shifted against me and pulled me closer. Flesh to flesh. Skin to skin. His face nuzzled against the back of my neck. I felt his lips brush against my nape. Hot breath and soft skin. The scruff of his beard tickled.

"Mmm," he murmured. His firm hand flattened against my stomach and pressed me to him. Morning's desire already teased us both. "We should do this more often ..." he said.

I smiled and closed my eyes, relishing the feel of his warmth.

"I have a deadline ..." I objected, but there was no conviction in my words.

I felt him nod behind me as his hand slid over my skin and gripped my hip, firm but gentle. "I know," he whispered.

"Malik is waiting on me ..."

He pulled back and placed his lips to my ear. "If I were the jealous type, I'd be concerned that you were thinking about another man while in my bed." His teeth nipped the edge there. Goosebumps rose on my exposed skin in response.

"I thought all Fae were jealous types." I sighed and reached back to thread my fingers into his curls.

"Mmmm ... true ... stereotypes exist for a reason." His lips kissed along my neck. "Be late," he whispered.

How could I say no?

Mean Girls

It was my office. My name was on the paperwork. There was a nameplate in the front foyer with an office name and number on it. Mine. Everyone in the building knew who I was and who it belonged to.

So why the hell was I standing in the Lobby, trying to figure out what the fuck was going on?

Beto dropped me in front of the Convention Center. I didn't need him to. I could get there on my own. However, the incident with Malik had, in fact, hit the feeds throughout the Kinship, and now everyone was on alert. My phone and his had blown up overnight, though neither of us cared to pay any attention. In retrospect, a couple of well-placed responses might have saved me from what I was currently facing.

Dropping me off was the better choice, given the options. If he had parked and walked me in ... while a chivalrous gesture ... one of these assholes would have decided that it meant that the Fae-Kin thought I couldn't take care of myself. Or I felt I couldn't trust the rest of them. Or I was making some grand gesture of partnership. Showing up on my own would have likewise fed the rumor-mill on why the man I was seen leaving with was not with me the next morning. I could go on for hours on the "what-if" scenarios that the Kinship would have come up with. It was like sitting at a table full of mean-girls in a High School lunchroom.

Twenty-some-odd Kin filled the front foyer of the Convention Center. My office was across from the Starbucks. Once upon a time, a Credit Union had a satellite branch here. Murr had booted them in the late '90's and moved the City offices there. In the Convention's Center, the middle of the visitor hub, right on the monorail. All paths led here eventually.

Murr had his priorities on The Strip, money and tourism. Big money. Big Money. Big Money. That had been the face of the City when he wore it. I hated that concept. I hated what it did to the people in the City. I hated this location, but I hadn't found anyplace to move to just yet.

I sighed.

Ok, here we go.

Robert's car was not quiet, and he made no attempt at subtly as he pulled in and dropped me off in clear view of the entrance. Heads and attention all turned on me the moment I closed the car door and headed in. I turned my eyes on the people gathered, trying to determine who was here from which groups.

A contingent of Shifters stood together opposite my office door, clearly avoiding the throng of gathered Kin. They watched the group with eyes trained to discern threats from prey. One of them gave me the chin down head nod.

A pair of hemophage stood quietly next to a set of side doors that led deeper into the Convention Center. Well away from the sunlight that flooded the foyer. I remembered seeing them at Plazma the night before.

El. I reminded myself. That was the name that Malik had used for the woman that was part of the pair. She had traded her deep red suit for a pair of dark denims and a loose-fitting black shirt. Her partner was an androgynous looking blonde wearing a white t-shirt and motorcycle jacket.

Three Haunts ... Spirit-Kin, I reminded myself, took up positions in the corners of the foyer. Their otherworldly origins presented in their appearance and outward presentation. Bright pupilless eyes and dramatic clothing set them apart from the others. Many of them channeled ancient entities tied to the land or the people. These were the closest in existence to the City Shards, carrying knowledge and experience for generations. They each watched the assembled Kinship, almost as if in judgment.

A handful of humans, obviously sent here to be eyes and ears for the Kinship, mulled around the foyer. One of them looked like they were taking notes. For who, I did not know.

I saw no other Fae. I doubted it was because of a lack of interest and probably had more to do with the Laird denying them permission to do so. Tatiyana's support of the City would probably hinge entirely on the outcome of the sponsorship of the changeling child in her custody. Beto's intentional presence was all the statement I would probably see from them.

Silent and serene, a single figure stood out from the rest. She was an older Kin. She appeared to be in her early fifties, but with Kin, she could have been far older. Her hair was the steel and white that denoted both age and mysticism. She wore a simple white cotton blouse and black trousers. Around her neck was an ornate necklace of silver, turquoise, and coral beads. It looked Nepali. A pair of hammered copper bracelets adorned her right wrist, and a woven red cord was worn on her left. She stood in a comfortable position, elbows resting at her sides, hands held before her, fingers steepled.

Amrita.

She was the only other Hex-Kin in the City. Or at least the only other one that I was aware of.

She was clearly here to talk about Malik.

As I crossed the threshold, it was as if I had stepped on a pressure-activated plate that set off a room full of animatronic figures. I was suddenly surrounded by faces, bodies, and voices.

"Is everything all right?"

"We heard about the incident."

"They can't treat you like that."

"You deserve better."

"Come by and let's talk."

"Ignore them. We know how to take care of you."

"Tell me what you need and I'll make sure you get it."

"You poor thing."

"I hope he treats you right."

"You can do better than him. "

"Call me."

"Come by and visit."

It was a cacophony of platitudes, requests, and passive aggressive nonsense. Like wading through a press conference. Questions, comments, gestures, requests. I nodded and smiled and accepted business cards as they were thrust into my hands and into my pockets. I was going to have to empty everything and check for personal messages, tokens of affection and talismans when all was said and done. While I may not be affected by them, they could still slip things onto my person, which allowed them to watch me remotely. Or track me. Like a supernatural GPS.

So annoying.

I took careful note of which Kin engaged in the various activities and which held back. I might be more inclined to speak to those later, over the ones clamoring for attention and favor. Respect for space was a thing.

I walked past Amrita. Her eyes met mine, and she smiled gently.

"When the City has the time, I am here for you," She said. Without further exchange, she made her way out.

Hex-Kin were the only ones who could hold the position of Librarian. If there were two in a city, it was because one of them was waiting for the other to fuck up. I knew exactly why she was here this morning.

That was a conversation I was not looking forward to.

The three Shifters remained gathered opposite the door to my office. They pushed off of the wall as the group that surrounded me approached. The largest of them, Andy Mak, was easily over 6 feet tall, broad and solid. He was rough around the edges. All of his edges. Frayed boot cuffs, a jacket that was worn at the elbows and neck. Dark stubble covered his lower face from a need to shave. His features were round, but his eyes and smile were sharp. He tipped his head as I approached. The pair that was with him both lowered their eyes.

"Kenny told us that Stratford was causing a ruckus." Mak's voice was deep and thick, like molasses. "You let us know if they need to be reminded of anything."

I rolled my eyes internally. One wrong step. One misplaced comment and the whole of this group would be on each other in a heartbeat. Meetings like this were dangerous, kept safe only because they were in a public venue and I was in the middle of them all. The only thing that kept them from tearing into each other here and now was the concern that one of them might accidentally cause me injury, and through that, injure the City. I dreaded to think what this area might have been like before there was a Shard here for them to want to protect.

I stopped walking. The throng that followed me peeled back as I turned to look at Mak and his companions. "Kenny talks too much," I replied simply.

Mak's eyes narrowed slightly. The other two Shifter-Kin with him seemed to bristle at the comment.

I stretched my neck a little and turned to look at all of them then.

Shard's got spice. Well, ok. Let's see what she's got today.

"There is an issue at hand with the Fae of the City," I said, loud enough to carry across the assembled group. "The Librarian and I had a difference of opinion last night on how I handled something pertaining to that issue."

Bodies shifted, comments were exchanged.

"This. Involves. None. Of. You." I said pointedly. I turned and looked at Mak. "Malik's issues with Robert Goode are his own. Beto is not involved in this. It is between Elegast and Scawen. "

At the mention of the two reigning nobles of the Fae-Kin, several of the Kinship groaned loudly. Their exasperation with Fairies clear. Mak's eyes narrowed deeper, his shoulders pulled back. He stared down at me.

"If those two shit in my pool, Shard Keeper, we are going to have a problem. We don't need their stupid ... games ... fucking up the City."

"I am aware, Mak."

"Are you?" he asked pointedly.

The din of conversation that had been filling the space dropped with the question. A blanket of strained silence filled it quickly. I suddenly felt someone standing at my side.

"Shard Keeper Hunter has a lot of business to attend to this morning." Malik's polite baritone broke the silence. I turned to look at him. He smiled back at me from behind his computer glasses. He reached out and offered me a cup. The smell of coffee and cinnamon wafted upwards. "Shall we?"

I nodded and accepted the coffee from the Librarian, and without further exchange, walked into my office and closed the door behind me.

"What. The. Fuck. Malik?" I asked as soon as the door clicked shut.

He nodded in agreement. His eyes darted to the door to the private office in the back. "I know, I know. I should not have said those things where the rest of the City could hear them ..."

I frowned. What the hell was going on?

"You are the Shard Keeper, after-all." His head tipped slightly toward the door as he slid around behind the desk in the front office. "Oh, your nine-o'clock is waiting in your office."

Nine-o'clock? I had a meeting? Malik was being very formal suddenly. I didn't like it.

"Thanks?"

"Sure thing. I've already settled her in. She was a little early." He offered a smile that said, I'm sorry.

Oh, fer the love of ... what was in my office?

I nodded and sipped my coffee as I headed for the back office. What fresh hell was waiting now?

The Laird of Las Vegas

The first time I met the Kinship of Las Vegas, I wasn't even old enough to drink. I would be in a couple of months, but for now ... I was twenty years old and couldn't even wander through most of the casinos without Dean in tow. I was a Junior College graduate with a degree in business standing in a room full of people that looked like they owned the world.

Expensive suits and dresses. High dollar hair cuts and top shelf cosmetics all the way around. My eyes were on their shoes. I remembered reading some study for my program about footwear being the tell for personality types. It was part of a section on interviews.

Reserved colors, but flashy footwear? Probably an extrovert.

Practical and functional? Probably laid back and easy-going.

Ankle boots? Watch your back, probably aggro.

It was weird, but that's where my head was when I walked into that room that night.

"Eyes up, Lyn. No time to be shy." Dean leaned in and whispered.

"Shoes," I replied.

"What?"

I looked up at him. "I was looking at their shoes for insight," I explained.

Dean's eyebrows rose a little. He nodded appreciatively. "Nice."

Dean wore dark brown bit-loafers. He was comfortable.

A pair of black and blue wing-tip derby shoes walked up to us. They were attached to a gentleman wearing a deep blue long coat and black trousers. An ornate gold brooch and chain adorned his left coat pocket, where a peacock's feather peaked out from the seam. He had dark hair and a close-cropped beard. Purple tinted glasses obscured his eyes.

"Dean." He met Dean's eyes and nodded simply.

"Sammy." Dean nodded back.

Sammy turned to look at me. Suddenly, I felt like the whole of my soul was being put under a microscope and being examined. I blinked. "Whoa. Not ok. Ask first," I said, holding up cautionary hands.

Sammy paused and pursed his lips in thought. "Interesting." He looked back at Dean. "She's sensitive. That's an unusual choice."

"She's also standing right here," I commented.

Sammy's right eyebrow quirked slightly. The right corner of his mouth lifted. "Outspoken. Not afraid to stand up for herself. That will be important," he observed. "I apologize. Is it 'she?' You are presenting female, but I should not presume, especially in this setting."

I paused. I had never thought about it before. "Uh, ya ... she is fine," I replied.

Sammy nodded. "Very good." He looked once more to Dean. "I like her. Good choice." Then the black and blue wingtips wandered back into the crowd.

"What the hell was that?" I hissed at Dean.

"That was your first interview," Dean replied.

After Sammy walked away, I stared at my reflection in the polished surface of a nearby pillar. Who was I tonight?

The face looking back at me was familiar, yet somehow different. Gone was the girl who'd stumbled into Dean's office all those years ago, to talk about her repeated issues in detention... replaced by someone who looked... older. More confident, maybe? But also more burdened.

I reached up to tuck a stray strand of hair behind my ear, a nervous habit I'd never quite shaken. The gesture was so normal, so mundane, it felt almost out of place in this glittering, supernatural world I now inhabited.

Just a year ago, my biggest concerns were running a cat cafe and figuring out how to pay off my student loans. Now? Now I was negotiating with creatures out of myth and legend, holding the fate of an entire city in my hands.

A wry smile tugged at my lips. "Bet you didn't see this coming, did you, Tam?" I muttered to my reflection.

I thought back to the cat cafe. Surrounded by the comforting purrs of rescued felines and the smell of freshly brewed coffee. It felt like a lifetime ago. I missed the simplicity of it, the straightforward joy of helping animals and making people smile.

But then I felt something else, a subtle awareness of the surrounding city. A faint pulse, like a second heartbeat, just beneath my own. It was overwhelming, terrifying... and exhilarating. For all the challenges and dangers that came with being the Shard Keeper, there was a part of me that couldn't imagine going back to my old life.

"You've got this," Dean's voice said from behind me. My eyes darted up in the reflection to find him watching me.

I took one more look at myself, adjusted my hair, and nodded.

"Right."

How much of the old me was about to walk out the door, never to be seen again?

Another pair of shoes walked up to greet us. Red soles. Louboutin.

Asshole.

It took a very specific type of person to pull off a corporate goth look and not come across as a bad vampire stereotype.

The woman sitting in the comfortable chair opposite my desk was such a woman.

Her hair was ink black, pulled into a long curled pony tail and accented with a short, blunt fringe of bangs. Her skin was impossibly porcelain and her lips were the bright, crisp red of fresh blood. She wore a white, high-necked ruffled blouse, a black corset jacket and pencil skirt. I expected tiny buttons running up the back seam of her skirt and kick pleat if she stood.

Next to her on the chair sat a wide-brimmed floppy hat and a black clutch purse.

My eyes landed on her feet.

Chunky-heeled platform Mary Janes. Not Louboutin.

Well, that was a statement.

"Your Grace," I greeted the Laird of Las Vegas politely.

"Shard Keeper," she replied. Her voice was like a soft summer rain.

She waited for me to round my desk and sit. I carefully placed my cup on a coaster on the expensive desk. "How can the City be of service to the Laird today?" I asked. Gloved hands carefully removed her large framed sunglasses, to reveal grey eyes with perfect wing tipped liner. "I believe we may have gotten off on the wrong foot when last we met." She carefully folded her sunglasses and held them in her lap.

The scar on my leg throbbed a little in response to the statement.

"Do tell." I reached for my coffee and sipped it as I watched her.

"I apologize for my outburst. It was ... hmm... uncalled for. Auberon, " She used one of Oberon's older names, "... brings the worst out in me sometimes. When you have been with someone as long as we were, you learn each other's hot buttons."

I said nothing and continued to sip my coffee.

"I understand he has given you a ... date for delivery... on the child?"

Now, how did you hear about that? I wondered.

"He has."

She nodded. "You cannot give the child to him, Shard Keeper."

"I don't know that there really is anything I can do about that, Your Grace ..."

"How is Hob?" she deflected.

I frowned.

"Ah yes, I forget. Dear Robin, how is he?"

Oh, this is where we were going to go.

"He's fine. You could call him yourself, and have that conversation, you know."

The Laird and Oberon's heir had not spoken politely with one another in years. I knew this.

"I doubt he'd answer, but I will keep that in mind. Thank you," she replied casually. "He's Auberon's oldest, you know."

"I am aware."

"The first child he ever stole from humanity."

The comment caught me off guard. That story did not match with what I had been told. "I thought he was tithed?"

"It's easier to think that, I'm sure." She tapped her glasses on her lap. "It's what he does, Keeper. Steal children. Steal ... humans ... and create changelings from them." She looked up at me then, ancient eyes filled with memories I could never know. "He deprives them of their mortality and their families, in the name of ... Fae."

She watched my face a moment and then looked away. "I'm sure he'll find someone with room in their home to take the child on, once all is said and done and he's increased our numbers by another mouth."

The idea sat poorly with me. I knew what it was like to be handed around from family to family. An Auntie taking me in, who did not plan on having a child and did not really want one. Ending up in the system and jumping from home to home. Tatiyana implied that Oberon's entire plan was to do this to a child intentionally.

"And what future would you offer them?" I asked.

She looked back up at me then. "I would not Change them," she replied.

"I ... see."

"We do not need to invoke Change to empower a child with belief, Keeper." She sighed. "But this is a matter of some debate between myself and Auberon ... and one that I doubt we will ever agree upon... sadly." She smoothed her skirt and set her glasses back onto her perfect face, then stood and reached for her belongings.

"Was there anything else I needed to know, Your Grace?"

Tatiyana adjusted her floppy hat, which seemed the perfect accent piece to her ensemble. She turned to face me. "I'll not be handing the child over to you, to give to Him for Changing. While I will loathe the conflict created if I refuse to abide by territorial agreements, I simply cannot do it. I am sorry for the trouble that is about to befall you. It has been brewing for centuries. I will do my best to limit its harm to your person. You are truly not the target of this battle."

Taking the child from Tatiyana and giving it to Oberon had seemed the easy call originally. Now, I had to wonder if there might not be a better solution.

"Then help me," I suggested.

She paused and regarded me carefully for a moment. Her dark glasses hid the windows of her soul and any chance to judge her temperament.

"How?" came the simple reply.

"You are the Laird of Las Vegas! Surely you have a debt that you can call in over him?"

She was quiet for a moment, this statuesque figure in black and white. A portrait in ebony and alabaster.

"Speak with Nicky Botham," she replied quietly. Then turned and exited the office, a gentle breeze following in her wake.

I sat. The chair beneath me objected to my unceremonious flump. Fuck. I did not want to drag Nicky into this. She'd been through enough because of these two.

Knuckles rapped on the doorframe. I looked up. Malik was standing in the doorway.

"Look, about last night ..."

I shook my head. "No, you were right."

"Wait? I was?"

"Ya. It was a ballsy move, I admit, and one that could have cost a lot of lives. I was counting on Ambroginio to not be an asshole. I can't take chances like that with people's lives." I looked up at Malik. "I'm sorry."

"Well, Amrita will be disappointed."

I cocked an eyebrow and stared at Malik.

"She doesn't get to be a librarian." He beamed a huge geeky smile. I rolled my eyes and gestured to the chair opposite me.

"Ya, well, they can all place bets on other things, I'm sure. We have a bigger problem."

"Just another day in the Kinship ..." He sighed and sat.

I filled him in quickly on my exchange with the Laird. He listened intently, fingers steepled on the desk's surface, nodding occasionally. Once I was done, he pursed his lips in thought.

"Well, that would match with some stories we have on file for him ... Oberon ..." He leaned back in the chair and adjusted his glasses. "If this is the Fae-Kin that was called into being by the name of Elegast ... the name he is currently using as his surname ... then ... it's very possible that what she said is entirely truthful."

I rubbed my forehead. There was a sudden throbbing there. Why did I know there would be more to this? And why did it have to be in my City? Why couldn't this Old Country Kin have stayed across the water where he belonged?

"I'm going to regret asking, aren't I?"

"Fourteenth century ... maybe fifth century... depending on his actual origin."

"Say what again?"

"Well, I mean, there is no guarantee that it's the same Fae-Kin," Malik objected.

"You mean to tell me that the Court Consort of Las Vegas might be a fifteen hundred-year-old Fae-Kin?"

Malik shrugged a little.

"Maybe?"

I turned and opened the bottom drawer of my desk and pulled out a bottle of whiskey. I set the bottle of dark brown liquid on the desk between us.

Malik's eyes met mine.

"I'll get the glasses."

DaVinci's

DaVinci's was a makerspace on the east side of the airport. It was strategically placed between a Taco Hut and a Donut Palace Coffee shop. The industrial warehouse was fabricated from a huge Quonset hut frame and built out to accommodate a variety of crafts and tradespeople. The back third of the building was devoted to the automotive shop. The first floor housed woodworking and carpentry, as well as a small ceramics lab. The second floor was the home of the computer and electronics lab and the stitchers' guild.

The organizers of the makerspace had been vocational and trade school graduates who knew each other in High

School. They had won a sponsorship based on a business proposal they had all submitted as part of their senior project. "Why it's not rude to be mechanical" talked about the need for vocational and trade education and the importance of community support for folks who just wanted to fix their shit.

DaVinci's was born from that passion.

Malik and I had sat in the City office for hours, going over other options that we might have that did not involve talking to Nicky Botham. We could still try to get the favor for Ambroginio and get him to tell Tatiyana to hand the child over. But somehow, the knowledge of what was going to happen to that child, if placed in Oberon's care, did not sit well with either of us.

Oberon's books were tight. He bought and sold his favors regularly, never holding on to anything for more than a year. He hated having outstanding debts. That much was clear. The one debt that was still floating around that was of any significant value was this one. We weren't sure if it was because Nicky was intent on holding the debt over Oberon's head, they'd forgotten the debt existed, or Oberon was actually sorry for what he had done.

I did not relish having to bring this situation up with her.

There was always something going on at DaVinci's. Whether it was filled with a local group working on a project together, or someone building something for their home, or even just a local handyman trying to get a leg up on some things, the space was always occupied.

We pushed the door open and stepped inside. The sound of voices and tools filled the air. I could smell fresh sawdust from behind the closed doors of the woodshop, and mechanic's oil from the back of the space. From upstairs, I heard a sewing machine.

We walked to a workbench that served as a front desk. Malik pulled his wallet out and ran it across a scanner. The light flashed from red to green, signing us in as members.

"Malik!" a voice called from across the room.

A couple of faces looked up from their projects. Smiles and waves followed, and then they returned to their work at hand.

The voice belonged to a young black man in his early twenties. He wore carpenter pants and a tool belt. His shirt sleeves were rolled up to his elbows, and he wore protective work goggles to protect his umber brown eyes. He was lanky and tall, but moved with a confident stride.

"Quincey." Malik nodded and held out his hand.

Quincey accepted Malik's hand and shook it firmly. "We rarely see you down here. You come to teach a class?" the young man asked. His eyes glanced in my direction. He nodded politely. "Ma'am."

Did I just get ma'am-ed? Easy. It's because of who you are, not your age. Calm down.

Malik shifted a little uneasily and rubbed the back of his neck. "Not today, I'm afraid. Though I'd be happy to. Put me on the schedule and I'll make it happen." He smiled.

"Is that Malik Shah I see standing at my front door?!" a woman's voice shouted from the back. She was about Quincey's age, but shorter and rounder. Her tight orange curls bounced as she walked, boots stomping on the concrete floor. She opened her arms wide and engulfed the Librarian in a warm hug.

"Oof! Hi Cozy." Malik managed.

She released him and turned to me. "Keeper." She nodded politely. "Whatcha need?"

Malik looked over at me carefully, then back to Quincey and Cozy.

Quincey frowned at the hesitation.

"Is Nicky in?" I asked.

"Oh, hell no," Cozy objected. She placed her hands on her ample hips. "You leave my girl Nicky alone, Keeper."

Quincey folded his arms across his narrow chest and looked down at both Malik and me. "I know I can't interfere with City business ... which is what I assume this is?"

Malik nodded. "It is."

"Nicky and Tom are in the back. We just got a load of bikes in from the police impound. They are fixing them up for a raffle over at Veterans Trib."

I nodded solemnly and headed toward the back of the space.. "Thank you."

"Keeper." Quincey caught my sleeve with his fingertips as I passed. He was careful not to actually grab me. I looked up at him. "Is this about ... them?" he asked.

"Unfortunately," I replied.

Quincey pursed his lips and shook his head. "What do they want now?"

I paused and thought about how to answer his question. Quincey, Cozy, Tom, and Nicky were just regular people who had the misfortune of winning the attention of the Fae Courts once. One Midsummer Night after graduation had changed their simple lives forever. Now they were among the residents of the City who were painfully aware of the presence of the Kinship all around them. There had been two other members of their little band that night. Penny's and Francis' minds had broken under the strain of the information and experience, and they had been remanded to State care.

And Nicky had ended up in a tub of her own blood.

The way the story went, Goode had come to Murr that night to tell him that something had gone wrong, and he needed the Keeper's help to clean up a mess. Not a call that any Keeper ever relished. The call that said

"Hey, the Kinship got someone hurt … or killed … can you lend a hand so we don't have a riot and a repeat of the Inquisition? Thanks."

I would have suspected Beto's involvement, had I not known where he was the night all of this went down. With me. By a fire. On a dune.

This had all been Oberon's fuckery, and Murr hung it squarely on the King-Consort's head once all was said and done.

But that didn't undo what had happened.

The crew at DaVinci's had no love for the Fae Courts, and here I was, about to get them involved once more.

I took a breath and met Quincey's eyes. There was no point in lying to him. He'd earned the truth years ago. "I need help to stop a war."

Silence dropped between us as I stared up at the carpenter.

Suddenly, Cozy burst out laughing. It was a rolling belly laugh that made it hard for her to breathe. "Oh. Oh! Oh my. Come on, come on." She tapped Quincey on the shoulder and waved back toward the auto shop. "I gotta hear this," she said and headed back toward the back.

I looked at Malik, who shrugged.

A heavy metal wall separated the automotive shop from the rest of the space. A wide metal door, featuring a thick glass window, occupied the center of the wall.

The kind you might see at a mechanic's shop that led from the waiting room into the work area. Behind the glass, one could see the automotive and mechanic shop of DaVinci's. There were two bays, each with a lift and mechanic's bench. A series of hoses and hydraulic tools hung from various hooks. The rolling doors for both bays were open, flooding the workspace with light and fresh air. A single large tool chest occupied part of one wall for both bays to share.

Lined up in one bay were a dozen bicycles. Bent frames, missing wheels, twisted handlebars, mismatched tires. These bikes were a mess. Vegas PD often collected abandoned bikes and had them repaired and raffled off to local High Schools, so students and teens might have a means of ready transport. The monorail was nice, but not everyone worked along the Strip. DaVinci's had apparently agreed to do this batch.

Standing in the middle of the metal graveyard were two figures and a welding cart. The pair were both roughly the same height and same build. Both wore heavy welding boots, gloves, and visors. Both wore long-sleeved coveralls. Their visors were up.

One of them was using a thick bristle wire brush to scrub at a fresh weld and clear away the blue black residue from the flux. They were talking about something.

At the sound of the shop door opening, they both looked in our direction.

Tom and Nicky were brother and sister. Not twins, but they were remarkably similar in appearance. Both dishwater blonde, with desert tanned skin and eyes the color of a cloudless summer day. Tom's face wore dark stubble that begged to be shaved. Nicky had clearly rubbed her face with a greasy hand at some point recently. Their coveralls were well worn from many months of recent use.

The smiles they wore fell away when they saw me.

I hated that.

If we had run into each other down at No Quarters or Crazy Eights, it would have been different. We would have drinks and argue about who was paying for the next round. But I was here with Malik, unannounced, walking in with Quincey and Cozy in tow. It was City Business, and City business meant Kinship. And the Kinship was a sore topic.

Tom stood up straight and threw the bristle brush down on the cart. It clattered loudly. He stepped defensively in front of his sister.

"Uh uh." He shook his head as he tugged off his gloves. "No. I don't care what it is."

"Tom," Nicky interjected.

"No, Nick. Just No," he continued.

Quincey took a position next to the door and leaned there, watching. Cozy stood next to him, arms folded across her plush bosom. She nodded in agreement with Tom.

I reached out and placed a pre-emptive hand on Malik's elbow. He paused and looked over at me. I shook my head. This was my job, not his. Normally, Dean would have helped me through the introductory bits of being who and what I had become. But Dean wasn't here, so Malik had stepped in. The Librarian of the City was remarkably efficient with knowledge, and everyone knew him. It helped to get me in to meet with people that normally might have avoided me.

But I knew this crew, which made this situation even more difficult.

I looked over at Nicky. Her eyes met mine, sparking blue topaz, filled with unspoken words, wishes and regrets. She placed her gloved hand on her brother's shoulder and squeezed it. Then stepped away from him.

"I got this, Tommy," she said. Nicky pulled her gloves off and tossed them onto the cart, then removed her visor and hung it from the end of the workstation. She'd shaved the sides of her head and wore the remaining mohawk in a short ponytail that was secured at the back of her head.

Tom shook his head in disbelief. "This is bullshit, Lyn," he said, using my middle name.

"Trade places with me?" I countered.

He snorted and shook his head. "Hell no."

"Then I gotta play the hand they dealt me and hopefully make good choices. For all of us."

"Whatever." He threw his hands into the air and stomped over to where Quincey and Cozy stood. "Come on, let's give them the room," Tom said with some reluctance.

"I wanted to watch!" Cozy objected.

Malik watched me and Nicky and then stepped over to Cozy. "Hey, Coz. How about we go look at the class schedule and get me on the books for the next couple of months?" He smiled gently at her.

Cozy's eyes widened, and she smiled a bright, toothy smile, grabbing Malik's arm and dragging him back into the other room. Quincey and Tom followed.

The door closed behind them with a solid *thunk*.

Nicky chewed a little on her top lip and then looked over at me. "Is this a coffee, soda, or beer conversation?" she asked.

"Beer, definitely beer."

She nodded. "Figured." She turned and walked across the workshop to where a small dorm style fridge occupied space next to a worn out chair. She recovered a couple of dark brown bottles and tossed me one, then tapped the top of hers on a workshop bench. The cap flew off and across the room. Nicky drank deeply from the bottle.

"Ok, what do I need to know?"

Elegast

I'd known Nicky Botham in High School. We'd come up together. Me and Nicky and Tom. For the few years we were at the same school, at least. Nicky and Tom transferred out to Veteran's Tribute Vocational the summer between Junior and Senior year. We kept in touch through the library. Neither of our families could afford cell phones for teenagers. That was not happening.

Nicky and her crew won their sponsorship and formed DaVinci's.

I graduated and went to Junior College under the watchful eye of Dean Franklin. I look back on it now and realize that maybe we all should have been a little more suspicious of the good fortune that seemed to fall on us all at the same time. We were all being steered by the Kinship.

That much was clear to me now.

Nicky and I leaned against the workbench after I explained what was happening, drinking in silence.

"He's a douche," she quipped.

I nodded in agreement. "No argument. Especially if what she said is true."

Nicky frowned a little and wiped her mouth with the back of her hand. The flash of a tattoo on her scarred wrist caught my eye. A semi-colon. A visual reminder to herself that her story was not yet over.

"I don't want to get involved in this, Lyn. You know that."

I nodded once more. "And I did not want to come here."

"And there really isn't anyone else you can go to?"

I shrugged. "Maybe? If I had more time to research it, I could find someone. But I have less than two weeks."

Nicky closed her blue eyes and lowered her head. She looked defeated. It killed me to see it and killed me twice over for being the one responsible for it.

"Would it be that bad?" she asked quietly.

"What?"

"Would it be that bad if you just let them go at each other?" She opened her eyes and looked over at me. "I mean, maybe she ends him and then we don't have to deal with his bullshit anymore."

"And maybe she doesn't … and then where are we?" I asked.

"Fuck, Lyn!" She slammed her free hand onto the workbench and stood. "Do you realize what happens if I do this?" She slammed her free hand onto the workbench and stood. She stared at me, eyes wide, unshed tears brimming there. "I open myself up to being screwed with again … by something I have no way of defending myself against." She shook her head and tossed her empty bottle into a bin. It crashed loudly, the sound of shattered glass echoed off the metal walls.

"I know."

"No. No, you don't, Lyn. And you never will. That's the problem," Nicky replied. "You're the Shard. Their … woojie … does not affect you. But it affects the rest of us … and they don't give a shit."

"That's not entirely true, Nick."

There were Kin in the City who were actively involved in the sponsorship and bettering of humanity. They weren't all self-absorbed narcissists like Oberon.

"Well, you find one of them that will defend me against the wrath of the Fairy King for forcing his hand. Then you come see me. Until then I gotta be a hard pass. I'm sorry." Her eyes met mine once more. I could feel the sorrow from ten feet away.

I looked away and down at the bottle in my hand. I couldn't force her to do it. And she was right. Oberon would come for her in a way that legends would not give justice to. I had to find another way.

I swirled the bottle, watching the contents for a moment, then lifted the bottle to my lips, drained it and set the empty on the workbench.

"I'll get it sorted." I nodded.

Wiping my hands on my pants, I looked over at Nicky. "See you down at Crazy Eights?"

She nodded absently, her thoughts clearly elsewhere. "Sure."

There was nothing left to say, so I showed myself to the door.

I remember the first time I met Oberon Elegast. It was at a New Year's party. A masquerade.

I was the newly minted Shard of the City. The ceremony had occurred on the 21st of December, ten days earlier. It was a smaller event than tonight. More intimate. There was a sense of exclusivity to it all. Leaders of the Kinship only. It made sense, limiting witnesses to the ceremony. I mean, to allow the whole of the Kinship to witness the process would have required us to hold the event at some place like the Thomas and Mack. I'm not even sure if the twenty-thousand seat arena there would accommodate them all, honestly. It would have also allowed people to interfere with the transference. Dean had assured me that there was nothing they could have done to prevent it, but somehow I doubted the shadow in his eyes when he said those words.

I was still reeling from the weight of it all.

I have to hand it to Shakespeare. Masquerades were a great way for people who might not otherwise talk to each other to do so openly. All under the guise of pretend identities. What was the term ... plausible deniability? I had to wonder whether most of these people realized that the anonymity they were hoping for could also be found in a dimly lit club, with alternating lights, loud music and dark alcoves.

Tonight would be the first night that the assembled Kinship got to see what the Shard had chosen for its next incarnation. Dean clarified that there were no limitations on what I wanted. Whatever the Shard wanted, there was a crew ready to build it and have it ready by New Year's. It was the most surreal experience I had ever had. But I ...knew... what I needed to wear without hesitation.

Pants. It had to be pants. I knew that. But it needed to make a statement. Now I stood in the Top of the World, overlooking the city, feeling every bit like Cinderella in an outfit that was made from wishes and dreams. A black jumpsuit, crafted to my measurements that exposed my left shoulder and the tribal ink I had done on my 18th birthday. A sheer, full train attached at the waist flowed gracefully to the floor, like a black waterfall. It was simple and unadorned, yet made all the statements it needed to without embellishment. The adornments came in two places. The shoes I wore were silver Latin ballroom heels, with sturdy heels, a delicate ankle strap and decorative beadwork. Flashy, but sturdy and meant to dance. And finally, my mask.

A white domino mask with wide black circles surrounding the eyes. Around these were intricately painted miniature flowers, no larger than the tip of my pinky finger. Purple and gold iris'. A delicate blue flower blossomed across the forehead of the mask, spreading out to reach the eyebrows. A crown of fresh, multicolored flowers outlined the top of the mask and wove into my hair. Blossoms the size of my fist. From this crown of life, sprung a dozen golden points, like rays of the sun. Each could be wielded as a weapon in a pinch.

It was La Catrina. The Lady of the Underworld. Typically, she would have been worn on the Day of the Dead, but something had told me that her visible recognition was the statement that the City wanted to make.

And what a statement it had been.

August Murr had been smiles and handshakes, drinks and deals in the back room. I was not the same Shard.

This Shard acknowledged the glitz of the Strip, the pageantry, the formal need for business deals, but also demanded the respect of the land upon which it was all built. It was something the Kinship was unprepared for.

I watched as the gathered Kin mingled and spoke with one another. Occasional furtive glances were sent in my direction and then they returned to their conversations. I quietly sipped the glass of red wine I had been handed, exchanging the rare pleasantry with the staff who came by to check on me.

"They are terrified of you," a deep baritone voice said from my left. I turned my head to look over and up at the figure standing there.

He was over six feet tall. Long ebony hair cascaded down his head and over his shoulders. Tiny strands of silver, wispy like spider silk, threaded through his onyx mane. His skin had a strange green tint to it. At first I thought it was body paint, but then I realized it was simply his. His eyes were dark, and seemed without distinct definition, as if hidden behind shadows. The velvet burgundy long coat he wore was worn open, the cut of his muscled form on obvious display. Hints of vine work tattoos teased beneath the coat edges along his ribs and across his tight stomach. From his brow sprouted a pair of impressive antlers. They curved out, up and around, entwining with one another and forming something that resembled a crown.

With a simple, graceful gesture, he offered me a single white rose.

"They don't appreciate the beauty of fear."

I hesitated for a moment before accepting the rose. Its petals were cool against my fingers, impossibly perfect. "And do you?" I asked, meeting his gaze.

His lips curved into a smile that was equal parts charming and predatory. "Fear, like respect, must be earned. You, my dear, have done just that."

I felt a shiver run down my spine, unsure if it was from his words or from the city responding to his presence. "I'm not here to be feared," I said, surprised by the steadiness in my voice. "I'm here to maintain balance."

He chuckled, a sound that seemed to resonate with the very foundations of the building.

"Balance, fear, respect - they are all intertwined in our world. You'll learn that soon enough." He paused, his eyes roaming over my costume. "La Catrina. An interesting choice."

"The city chose it," I replied, my fingers absently tracing the edge of my mask.

"Did it now?" He seemed genuinely intrigued. "And what else has the city told you, I wonder?"

I felt a surge of defiance. This was Oberon Elegast, I realized. The Fairy King of Las Vegas, and he was trying to gauge me, to find my weaknesses. "I think," I said carefully, "that's between me and the city."

His eyes flashed with something - approval? Amusement? - before he inclined his head slightly.

"Well played, Shard Keeper. I look forward to seeing how you navigate our little world."

He took a step closer, and I caught the scent of earth and ozone. "A word of advice, if I may. The crown you wear - both this one," he gestured to my floral headdress, "and the metaphorical one - they are beautiful. But beauty often hides thorns. Be prepared for the weight of it, and for those who will try to take it from you."

With that, he gave me a small bow and turned to leave. "Until we meet again, La Catrina. May your reign be... interesting."

As I watched him disappear into the crowd, I realized I was clutching the stem of the rose tightly, its thorns pricking my skin. A single drop of blood welled up, stark against my palm.

I looked out over the city again, its lights now seeming both more vibrant and somehow more ominous. Oberon's words echoed in my mind. The weight of the crown, indeed. I straightened my shoulders, feeling the responsibility of the Shard settling around me like a cloak.

Whatever challenges lay ahead, whatever games the Kin might play, I would face them. For the sake of the city, for the people who called it home, I had to.

Push and Pull

That same ebony-haired figure stood in my offices upon my return. A perfectly chiseled statue carved from the flesh of the forest itself. Where the Laird had adopted modern fashion trends, her Consort maintained a more ... traditional ... display.

His long flowing coat, crafted from silk brocade in forest greens, opened down the front to reveal a sheer white poet's shirt. Long lace draped effortlessly from its wide bell cuffs. Black leather pant legs were tucked into thigh-high boots with bright gold buttons down the sides. Ivy curled around his antlers. He was a picture from a mythology book. Or the cover of a romance novel.

Malik bristled a little at the presence of the Fae Consort. We had locked the offices when we left earlier.

"I'm sorry, Your Highness, did you have an appointment?" he asked as we crossed the threshold. He did not wait for an answer, but walked around the reception desk and flipped through the calendar there.

"I was in the neighborhood," Oberon replied with a casual wave of his long-fingered hand. The shadows that served as his eyes seemed to look in my direction. He inclined his head politely.

"May the City ever flourish."

A shiver crawled up my spine and blossomed across my shoulders at Oberon's words. It was not an unpleasant sensation. While I was not susceptible to their magic, the Shard was still tied to the Kinship of their territory. Deference and blessing were something I could feel on my skin and in my soul.

The left corner of Oberon's mouth quirked upward slightly at my uncontrolled response.

"May peace and prosperity endure," I replied. It was the expected answer to his blessing.

Oberon inhaled deeply, a broad smile breaking across his features.

"She was here. Excellent," he commented. Tatiyana's perfume still lingered in the room from earlier in the day.

He raised the fingers of his right hand and examined his nails carefully. "She has seen reason finally, then?"

"Her Majesty makes no concessions," I replied, careful not to flavor my response with anything other than neutrality.

Oberon dropped the hand he had been examining and turned his attention back to me. His head turned and tilted, heavy antlers caused the bands of muscles down his neck and across his shoulders to tighten to accommodate the gesture.

"Oh, rash wanton wife ... what news is this then?" he murmured. "She declines?" he asked simply.

"At this time," I replied.

A deep chuckle echoed in Oberon's chest. "A fortnight yet remains for her mind to change ... or be changed ..." His attention focused on the ceiling for a moment. His shoulders rose and fell in a shrug. "No matter. She will come to see things my way." He looked back in my direction. The hint of a smile tugged at the left edge of his mouth. "She always does."

I really hated this guy.

"As you say."

Oberon stood there a moment, regarding me carefully. The aura of centuries ebbed and flowed around him. He felt timeless. It was power. Refined. Honed. Effortless. He was terrifying and awe-inspiring.

"Kenny Yazzi is on his way down, Tam." Malik's voice broke the ancient Fae Lord's glamour.

Oberon's eyes twitched slightly in irritation. He turned away from me to focus on Malik. "Is the flea-ridden Coyote departing his kennel?"

Relationships among the Kin varied from group to group and City to City. In some areas, the Fae were allied with the Shifters, in others, they were allied with the Spirit or Hex-Kin. Depending on the Fae types in the area, they may even be allied with the Blood-Kin. Those were often dark and dangerous members of the Kinship, paired for their nightmarish similarities. Here, the Fae and the Shifters were not on the best of terms.

In truth, the Fae-Kin of Las Vegas were not loved by most of the Kinship of the City.

Standing here with Oberon now, I could understand why.

I straightened my shoulders and looked up at the Lord Consort. "Yazzi and Mak, and the rest of the Shifters of the City have an equal voice in this City, as well as an equal right to petition... Your Highness."

Oberon's lips curled into a distasteful grimace, revealing the hint of sharp teeth. "There was a time when the animals remembered their place in the enclave." His voice was soft, almost wistful, but laced with venom.

"And a time when yours remained in your earthen work tunnels unless summoned," Malik interjected.

My eyes darted to where Malik stood. The normally quiet and demure Librarian of the City had taken an aggressive posture. His glasses were set aside on the top of the work desk and he had loosened the top two buttons of his shirt. An intricate gold medallion rested against his bronze toned flesh. His amber eyes focused on the figure of the Fae Lord as he slowly rolled up his right sleeve.

The air crackled with unspoken threats and centuries-old grudges. I could almost see the invisible lines of power being drawn across the room, like a chessboard coming to life.

Malik stood silently, his posture rigid but controlled. His eyes, usually warm and kind, had hardened into chips of amber. I could see the struggle in him, the effort it took to maintain his composure in the face of Oberon's taunts.

Oberon's gaze slid from me to Malik, a cruel smile playing at the corners of his mouth. "Tell me, Librarian," he purred, his voice dripping with false sweetness, "how many tomes have you collected on the burning of cities? I hear Xativa has quite the... extensive history in that regard."

I saw Malik flinch, as if he'd been struck. His face paled, and for a moment, I thought he might be ill. But then color flooded back into his cheeks, and his eyes blazed with a fury I'd never seen before.

"You dare…" Malik's voice was barely above a whisper, but it carried the weight of eons. His hands, usually so steady, trembled at his sides.

Oberon's smile widened, revealing more of those unnaturally sharp teeth. "Oh, I dare much, little keeper of books. After all, what are a few charred pages in the grand scheme of things? Though I suppose the screams of the dying make for poor bedtime reading."

Something in Malik snapped. The careful control he'd maintained for so long shattered like glass.

His glasses clattered to the desk as he surged forward, loosening his shirt with trembling fingers. The intricate gold medallion at his throat gleamed in the office lights, seeming to pulse with its own inner fire.

"Avekan," he whispered, the word reverberating with power.

The smell of ozone filled the air, laced with the rich scent of frankincense. Golden light coalesced around Malik's left arm, forming intricate, swirling patterns.

Oberon's eyes widened fractionally, a flicker of surprise crossing his features before being replaced by a predatory grin. "Oh, my dear Librarian," he purred, drawing himself up to his full, imposing height. "I thought you'd never ask…"

"Accipio," Oberon replied with a flourish. As he completed his movements, he drew a wicked-looking blade from the shadows. It solidified into a weapon crafted entirely of onyx glass.

As Oberon spoke his acceptance of the challenge, I realized with growing horror that I was about to witness a magical duel in the middle of my office. The tension that had been building had finally found its release, and Malik–steady, dependable Malik–had been the one to strike the first spark.

Holy fuck, they were going to throw down in the middle of my office.

My eyes widened as I realized what was about to happen.

Malik's left arm glowed as golden power solidified around it in an intricate design. The fingers of his right hand moved, stretching, jerking, and twisting in arcane symbols. He mouthed silent syllables that burned on the air.

Oberon crouched, a great predator ready to leap from the shadows on its prey. His onyx blade held at the ready. Darkness danced around his ancient form, teasing at the light and distorting his figure from clear view. I could feel him chuckling.

I looked around the office for some place to take cover. I didn't have many options. Walls of glass and metal. A couple of chairs. Malik stood behind the heaviest piece of furniture in the room. Oberon blocked the doorway to my private office.

Not helpful.

Superhero style video games sometimes give you enough time to prepare to react to an incoming assault from the antagonist. There's music. Big build up. Drama. None of that happens in the real world.

I didn't have time to choose where I needed to be before the first blast of magical energy erupted from the Librarian. Light sizzled and burst from Malik's left hand. It reminded me of something from a science fiction movie. The light passed through the space where Oberon had been and slammed into the closed door there. The door exploded into charred splinters.

I covered my head with my arms, ducked and darted behind a chair as pieces of the door and doorframe rained down around us.

Lights flashed and horns blared as the fire alarm system kicked over in response. Seconds passed. Then the water kicked in.

The shadowy figure of the Consort was nowhere to be seen. He had been there one moment, and now he was gone.

Through the glass walls of the office, I saw people pushing each other in a hurried exit toward the doors of the convention center. The occasional pair of eyes turned in our direction before being swept away in the wave of bodies.

Shadows flickered in the corner of my eye. Something moved across the ceiling.

The chill of his presence ran up my spine before I felt him behind me. Strong fingers wrapped around my wrist and hauled me to my feet. His left arm moved to wrap around my waist and pulled me against him, his chest to my back. He smelled of rich earth and damp moss.

"Tsk, tsk, tsk," Oberon's deep voice clucked. He brought his onyx bade up before us both.

His cold lips brushed across my ear. "You place too much faith in a man who let Xativa burn," Oberon whispered.

Across from us, Malik's eyes widened. He blanched.

"Tam," he whispered.

The magics that fuelled the Librarian's figure fell away, like cotton candy melting in the rain. He held his hands up, palms open. A gesture of surrender.

Oberon twisted his right wrist and brought the tip of his blade forward to point it at Malik. "So much passion. So little forethought. Some things never change, do they, Librarian?" Oberon's arm squeezed around my waist, almost possessively. "Remember who kept you safe on this day ... Shard Keeper." In a practiced maneuver, Oberon twirled me toward Malik and stepped backward to disappear into a blossom of shadows.

I stagger-stepped forward and fell into Malik's out-stretched arms. He caught me and pulled me in, arms cradling me. He turned us both away from where Oberon had been standing, shielding my body with his.

But there was no response.

Oberon Elegast was gone.

I found my words after a few seconds.

"Let me go."

Malik pulled back and helped us both to a standing position. Ozone still burned in the air. It was coupled with smoke and the scent of burned wood. The blinking lights and roaring alarm bells filled the office.

I could see people running past the office, headed for the outside doors. Once in a while, I could see the flash of a camera.

Dammit.

The air still crackled with ozone, mixed with the acrid scent of smoke and charred wood. Blinking lights and blaring alarms filled the office, disorienting in their intensity.

Through the glass walls, I saw people fleeing, some paused to snap photos with their phones. Great, just what we needed–a social media frenzy.

"Malik, shut off that damn alarm!" I shouted over the cacophony. He nodded, darting to a control panel and inputting a series of commands. The horns fell silent, though the lights continued their frantic dance.

The wail of approaching sirens cut through the relative quiet. I knew what came next. Kneeling in the foyer, I crossed my ankles and raised my hands, praying Malik had the sense to do the same.

The door burst open, a flood of uniforms pouring in. Rough hands grabbed my wrists, forcing me face-down.

"I'm Tamara-Lyn Hunter. This is my office!" I called out, fighting to keep my voice steady. "My ID's in my back pocket. The man is Malik Shah, my assistant. We are unarmed!"

A scuffle behind me told me Malik wasn't faring much better. I bit back a curse. The Kin knew who we were, but to the human authorities, we were just suspects at a crime scene.

Heavy footsteps approached. I looked up to see black boots and tan pants with reflective stripes. A familiar voice boomed above me.

"What the hell is this?"

Relief washed over me. Andy Mak. At least someone here knew what was really going on.

"Explosion reported, Captain. Found these two inside," came the reply from one officer.

"Yeah, no shit. They work here," Andy growled, crouching down to meet my eyes. "You okay, Keeper?"

I nodded, grateful for his presence. As Andy helped me up, memories of our first meeting flooded back.

He'd been intimidating then, all raw power and sharp edges. "So you're the new Keeper," he'd said, sizing me up. "Hope you're ready for this, kid. Vegas doesn't play nice."

I'd put on a brave face. "I can handle it."

His laugh had been more growl than chuckle. "We'll see."

Over the years, I'd come to respect Andy's leadership. He'd united the Shifter clans of Vegas–no small feat given their territorial nature. Wolves from the desert outskirts, big cats prowling the Strip, even the watchful ravens perched on skyscrapers–all answered to Andy Mak.

Now, as he turned to address the surrounding chaos, I saw the same fierce determination that had propelled him to power. Andy wasn't just a leader; he was a protector, devoted to his people and his city.

"Keeper," he growled, pulling me from my reverie. "This Fae bullshit is getting out of hand. My people are restless. We need answers."

I nodded, understanding the gravity of his words. If Andy was worried, things were dire indeed.

"I know, Andy," I replied, keeping my voice low but firm. "We're working on it. But I need you to keep your people in check. The last thing we need is widespread panic."

His eyes narrowed, but he gave a curt nod. "You've earned our trust, Tamara. Don't make me regret it."

As he turned to deal with the officers, I caught sight of his forearm tattoo—a stylized paw print encircled by symbols of Vegas' Shifter clans. A reminder of the unity he'd forged and the responsibility he carried.

"Bitsko, get off him! He's a damn secretary!" Andy's voice boomed as he strode to where Malik was still being restrained.

A crackle of radio chatter, then: "They check out, Cap. Station says to hand it off to fire crew, possible arson investigation to follow."

The officer who'd pinned me helped me up, mumbling an apology. I watched as Andy assisted Malik, who seemed unsteady on his feet.

"Get him outside and checked out," Andy ordered one firefighter, who quickly complied.

Turning to the overzealous officer, Andy's voice dropped to a dangerous growl. "Bitsko, you know damn well whose office this is. Get out of my sight."

The man paled, muttering another apology as he retreated.

I surveyed the wreckage of my office—shattered door, water damage from the sprinklers. It would take weeks to sort out this mess with insurance and repairs.

And I had less than two weeks to resolve the Elegast situation. With no neutral ground left for negotiations.

God Damn It.

The Weight of Obligation

"The offices of the Keeper are neutral ground. Every voice has a right to be heard there." Dean lectured. I hadn't really been paying attention, though. I had been thinking about a bon fire and sand buggy.

Suddenly there was a hand in front of my face, and fingers snapping loudly. "Earth to Lyn. You in there?"

I blinked and refocused. "Ya. Ya. I'm here." I clicked the pen in my hand and jotted down some notes. "Shard space is like Switzerland. Got it."

Dean leaned his hip against the edge of the counter and regarded me for a moment. Eyes that had clearly seen too much for a single lifetime searched me for information.

I scowled. I didn't want to get him involved in any of this. I certainly didn't feel comfortable telling him about what had happened. It would have been like talking to your dad about a first date.

Awkward.

Dean must have picked up on the discomfort, because he nodded quietly. "You .. ah... hmm... you still wanna go through with this? Still time to change your mind," he finally asked.

"What? No, that's not it!" I shook my head firmly. I stretched and stood. "Just tired, that's all." I walked away from the table and behind the counter. Pulling down a pair of cups, I gestured at the coffeepot. Dean nodded. I poured two and slid him one.

"You were working the clean-up crew last night, weren't you?" He tore open a pink packet of fake sugar and poured half of it into his coffee.

"Yup."

"Everything go ok?"

"Yup."

"You wanna talk about it?" he asked quietly.

"Nope." I shook my head and tried to ignore the request.

"You sure? You know you can talk to me," he offered again.

I lifted my cup to my lips and blew across the hot brown liquid. "I'm fine, old man. So, what happens if someone breaks that neutrality?" I changed topics.

Dean regarded me a moment more, then nodded in acceptance of the fact that I was not budging on the topic. I knew that just meant he would make calls to the organizers and check up on what happened. This was my life now.

Supernatural politics.

Living in a fishbowl.

And the ceremony hadn't even happened yet. I wondered if this was part of the whole test. Can the Keeper handle the constant questions and being observed? Can you accept that your life will never really be yours again?

It was a lot.

Dean blew out loudly in response to the question. "Well ... it's not good," he started.

"So descriptive. Care to elaborate, Captain Dodge-the-Question?"

He set his cup down and rubbed his jaw with his hand in thought. "It's not like there's some mystical force involved..."

"Oh! Well, that's good to know. Something that might just be normal in all of this?"

He scowled at me. I looked away.

"You know how there are just some places that society tells you are areas you protect and things you don't do?

Like … like eating potato chips in the middle of a library and wiping your greasy fingers on the pages of a book…"

"Damn, even I wouldn't do that."

"It's kinda like that."

I considered Dean's words as I sipped my coffee and leaned on the countertop of the cafe. It had been a quiet evening. The Yoga-With-Cats class had ended an hour ago, and everyone had cleared out shortly thereafter. It was still a weird concept for me. A cat-cafe. But who was I to judge? It paid my bills and gave me autonomy enough to have weird-ass conversations about the supernatural like it was a common everyday thing.

Which, I suppose it was. Just not something everyone knew about.

In comparison, the cat-cafe suddenly seemed way more normal.

"Ok, so what are we talking about? Fines? Mystical grounding for two weeks? You said it wasn't good. The most I had to deal with was dirty looks from Ms. Spencer and $20 fine for a lost book."

Dean rubbed the side of his face with an open hand. I could hear the stubble, it sounded like sandpaper.

"If the area is not damaged and it can still be used? Ya, favors could be paid out to the aggrieved parties, which could put someone in debt for a very long time."

"And if it is damaged?"

"If the area can no longer be used to serve as a neutral meeting area for the Kinship," Dean paused and looked directly at me. He looked grim.

"Banishment."

The headache I had from dealing with Nicky at DaVinci's earlier was nothing compared to the icepick that was currently wedged in my right eye socket, named Oberon.

Bodies surrounded me as we stood in the damaged offices of the Convention Center. Representatives from the entire Kinship tried to squeeze into the space that had once been my office. Body odor mingled with sweat and the musky aroma of mold that was already forming in the summer heat flooded my nostrils. I stood behind the desk in the foyer. The massive wooden artifact was currently serving as a barrier between myself and the very irritated supernaturals who were vying for attention at the moment.

Concern for the Shard, anger at the assault on the office, frustration at the loss of neutral territory, demands for action. I felt like I was standing in the middle of a PTA meeting, and the choir teacher for the Junior High had just suggested the school put on a performance of *Jesus Christ Superstar*.

"This is completely unacceptable," a refined voice spoke. "The City cannot be expected to host conferences under these circumstances."

"It is an insult." Another voice agreed.

They sounded like mothers arguing over wedding plans and seating assignments.

"Shah needs to be held accountable. He did this."

"It's Xativa all over again."

There was that reference. I'd heard it twice before in recent days. It had been what set Malik off. Comments that seemed aimed at Malik Shah, the Librarian of the City. References to something he had allowed to happen centuries earlier. Ambroginio and Oberon both implied that Malik had been responsible for the fall of Xativa back in the 1700s. Something about failure to inform the Kinship about allergies and the implication that the Shard Keeper had fallen ill under his watch.

Or was poisoned.

"It's fine," I mumbled.

"Keeper Hunter, I assure you it is not," that same refined voice objected. I recognized it. Sammy. My first interview.

I slowly lifted my eyes to meet theirs. They wore the same purple-tinted glasses they had worn the night of our introduction. Just dark enough to hide the pupilless eyes that were the telltale mark of spirit-kin. I knew Sammy channeled the soul of an ancient spirit, but I didn't know who. It had never come up in conversation.

"Khun Somchai," I used Sammy's formal name to address him. "I realize this situation is inconvenient."

"Inconvenient?" he blustered. "The inviolate has been violated!"

Tradition is vital to the existence of Spirit-Kin, I reminded myself. I continued to hold his eyes, ignoring the movements, comments and gestures from the other Kin around us. Somchai held my entire attention at the moment. It was a sign of respect for his people.

I slowly straightened my posture and placed my palms together at chest level and inclined my head politely. "And it shall be addressed."

Sammy halted his blustering demands at the gesture. It was simple, but also conveyed an understanding and respect for both his people, and the spirit that he carried within his body. I had to regain some semblance of order in the chaos' wake that Elegast left.

Sammy returned the gesture with a nod of his head and a lowering of his eyes. "As you say, Shard Keeper. May the City always thrive."

I felt a jolt of power that had no description flood through my form as a chorus of assembled voices echoed the statement. "May the City always thrive." It started at the base of my spine and blossomed upward and across my shoulders like a set of warm hands running up my body. For a moment, I was not me. I was a dozen distinct entities standing in my office. I was a young woman playing in the sprinkler across town. I was a pit boss watching someone counting cards. I was an older woman folding sheets in a hotel hallway. I was a performer doing a bump before a show. I was a doctor walking into a waiting room, a heavy weight of information on my heart.

It reminded me of the ties I had to the creatures standing here and beyond. For all their bickering and demands, they needed me, or their worlds would fall apart. Slowly, my sense of self returned to me. Many of those gathered seemed satisfied with whatever they felt on their end by the invocation. The sense of urgency seemed lessened.

I just needed to buy some time.

"We call for the removal of Malik Shah from his position as Librarian."

The buzz of conversation died in the room.

I recognized the owner of the voice before I saw him. I knew it better than any other voice in my current life. It was the voice I heard in the morning, and often the last one that I heard before I drifted off to sleep. It was comfort and consolation, protection and passion.

The sea of bodies parted like some choreographed movie scene as he walked into the room. My eyes drifted to the figure standing in the doorway, dressed in greens and golds, then dropped to his shoes.

Venetian Italian wingtips. Blucher and Cognac brown. Hand tooled. Bruno Magli.

Formal.

Timeless.

He only wore them when on business.

My eyes lifted from his shoes to his face. A face that I had committed to memory and had carved a space in my heart. His golden-green eyes were carefully masked from any emotion. This wasn't the man who had romanced me by a bonfire out on the dunes years ago. This was the timeless messenger of the Fae Courts. Come to discharge his duty of office before the Kinship.

"For the casting of violent magicks, which damaged the sacred spaces and threatened the safety of the Shard, and for an unprovoked assault upon the person of Oberon Elegast, does Tatiyana Scawen, Laird of Las Vegas, demand just satisfaction."

There was no time to be bought.

I stared at Robert Goodfellow, standing in his green suit with tiny gold pinstripes, his right hand clasping his left wrist as he stood in the middle of my flooded office. An office neatly destroyed by the manipulative actions of his father only an hour ago. A father who may have only been so in name, who may have stolen Robert's humanity and forced him to become as he was now.

Did it make him any less a father in Beto's eyes? I didn't know.

"Robert ..." I started.

"Seconded," a woman's voice carried across the room.

Heads turned, and eyes searched for the owner of the comment. Standing in the corner, her back to the wall, steel colored hair neatly pulled into a bun at the base of her neck. Her white silk suit meticulously pressed to perfection. A sheer scarf in a brilliant scarlet, embroidered in gold, draped effortlessly across her left shoulder and trailed toward the floor. Her feet were bare, adorned with golden toe rings and painted with intricate designs in henna.

I stared at them a moment, uncertain of how to process the very intentional statement. Humility or statement of strength?

I lifted my eyes from the feet of the older woman and met her chestnut brown eyes with my own. She smiled softly and inclined her head in deference.

Amrita.

The only other Hex-Kin in the City.

I nodded in silent acceptance.

"Bullshit!" Andy Mak's deep baritone broke the tension. "This is a fucking play and you know it, Keeper!"

Kin started at the abrupt comment. Many took positions of defense and ready. Sammy and one of his entourage moved around the sides of the desk to flank me. One of the Blood-Kin bore their fangs and hissed sharply at the outburst. Damage to the sacred space had already been done. There was nothing to stop them all from tearing into each other any longer.

In the middle of it all, Robert remained. Unflinching. Unmoved. A russet-haired god standing in a sea of uncertainty. A Fae-born creature riding the waves of chaos around him.

I looked in Andy's direction. He was already embroiled in an argument with a punk-rock clad Blood-Kin. Their threadbare black t-shirt depicted a skeletal hand in a throwing horns gesture. Nose-to-nose and toe-to-toe, two predators sizing each other up for weaknesses.

"Enough!" I shouted. The pain behind my eye throbbed abruptly. The Kinship must have felt it as well. They halted their actions and turned to look at me.

Calm and silence returned to the room.

"The complaint is heard from the Fae-Kin and seconded by the Hex-Kin. The remaining Kin of Las Vegas have until dawn tomorrow to consider the measure and return their vote to me from their appointed leadership." I looked at the expectant faces around the room. "All Kin present will leave now."

One by one, everything moved around me. Kin left the room, some in a rush, others with a few quiet words or gestures to those around them.

Only Robert remained, standing across from me. Clearly, he did not think my words applied to him. His green eyes were focused on a point across the room. I didn't speak to him. I was afraid that I would make the wrong decision in my emotional state. I had to figure out how to handle this.

After the last of the Kin were gone, I finally spoke.

"Your dad's a fucker, you know that?"

"Yes," he replied.

"What the hell did he say?" I asked.

"He made me an offer I couldn't refuse."

"Quaint. A hundred years ago? Four hundred?" I placed my hands on the surface of the desk before me. "Jesus, Beto, how do we get through this?"

"Carefully."

"That's not the answer I'm looking for, Robert."

"I know."

"You're gonna show up at my office, throw some Kin Law at me and walk away like you don't give a shit? After all I've just been through? After everything you and I have been to each other? Do you really think that's gonna work?"

He said nothing.

"I thought you were different from Oberon. Different from your father."

"I am his son, Tam," he said. "I am the result of his actions. I did not choose this path. I accepted it."

"You're still choosing it!"

"I do not have a choice in the matter." His voice was flat.

"Bullshit!" I shouted. "You're a fucking person, dammit! You're a goddamned individual!"

My torrent of emotions and words did nothing to him. I could not break the shell. Impotent in my own space.

"There are many things you do not understand about me, Tam," he said. "I have obligations you cannot understand." He took a step toward me. "Obligations that would be impossible for you to understand."

"And I don't?" I said. "I'm the fucking Shard Keeper, Robert! Don't come at me about obligations. The whole CITY depends on me!"

"You could have said no," he said. "All those years ago? When Dean came to you and told you everything? You could have said no and just gone on with your perfectly mortal life." He took a step toward me. "You could have easily left Las Vegas behind you. And yet you stayed…"

"You're right," I said. "I did."

"Why?"

That hit me. Like a punch in the gut. I could have walked away from all of this. I could have said no. I could have bailed. But I didn't. I said yes.

I looked up and into Beto's eyes.

"Do I need to say it?" I asked.

"Yes," he whispered.

"I couldn't leave. Because of you."

He smiled. "Then you are a fool, Tam. A fool for staying."

"I'm not a fool."

"A prisoner, then."

"No, Beto. I'm not a prisoner." I looked him in the eye. "I'm just in love with you."

Silence. But for the thrumming of my heart in my chest.

Our eyes locked on each other's as we stood in the destruction of my office. The remains of civility laid bare and broken around us.

"I'm sorry," he whispered. Then the Fae-Kin heir-apparent turned and walked away.

Bootstraps

Let's summarize the depths of the suck that I was currently neck deep in.

The Fae-Kin Lairds of the City were getting ready to take up arms over the tithe of a human soul. I had less than two weeks to solve their issues or they would tear the City apart warring with each other. The only neutral area in the City had just been destroyed by the tangential actions of one of those same parties. There was a distinct possibility that said destruction was an intentional maneuver, to remove the only neutral place for negotiations in the City. In the process, I had lost my chief ally and political navigator, who was also one of my only friends. The mortal friends I would like to go to for support were wrapped tip-to-tail in history with the aforementioned parties and wanted nothing to do with them ... or me, right now. On top of it all, the man I loved best in this world had reminded me he was not mortal and would always have obligations beyond me.

It's a bitter reality when you realize you really have no one but yourself.

As I stood in my ruined office, that truth hit me hard, dragging me back to another moment of crushing loneliness. That Tuesday. Just another day, until it wasn't.

I was knee-deep in paperwork when the phone rang. I almost didn't answer it.

"Is this Tamara-Lyn Hunter?" A crisp, professional voice asked when I picked up.

"Speaking."

"This is Desert Springs Hospital. You're listed as the next of kin for Franklin Dean."

The world tilted on its axis. Again. Just like it had when I was six and they told me my parents weren't coming home. Just like when I was eight and my aunt decided she couldn't handle me anymore. Just like every time a foster family decided I wasn't the right fit.

"There's been an incident. Mr. Dean suffered a massive heart attack. We did everything we could, but..."

The voice faded into a dull roar in my ears. I don't remember hanging up or leaving the office.

Somehow, I found myself at the hospital, staring at a body under a white sheet that couldn't possibly be Dean. Dean, who had guided me through the madness of becoming the Shard. Dean, who had been my rock, my compass in this insane world of Kin politics and supernatural bullshit.

Dean, who was now gone. Just like everyone else.

A nurse handed me a small box. "These were his personal effects," she said. Her eyes held that mix of pity and awkwardness I'd seen so many times before. The look that said, "I'm sorry for your loss, but I don't know how to handle a grieving person."

I opened the box later, alone in my apartment. The silence was deafening, broken only by the occasional car passing outside and the hum of the refrigerator. Sounds that seemed obscenely normal in a world that had just shattered. Again.

His watch. A folded handkerchief. A small, worn notebook. And a letter addressed to me. My hands shook as I unfolded it.

Tam

If you're reading this, well... I guess I finally kicked the bucket. Probably ate one too many of those greasy burgers you always nagged me about. I'm sorry I couldn't stick around longer. Being a Shard Keeper isn't easy, and I wish I could've been there to help you through it all. But you're strong, Tam. Stronger than you know. You've got this. Remember what I taught you: trust your instincts, keep your word, and never let the bastards see you sweat. The City chose you for a reason. Don't forget that. I know you've lost a lot in your life, kid. More than anyone should have to. But don't let it harden you. Your heart, your compassion - that's what makes you special. That's why the City chose you.

Take care of yourself, kid. I'm proud of you.
~Dean

I don't know how long I sat there, clutching that letter, tears silently streaming down my face.

The weight of responsibility, always heavy, now felt crushing. I was twenty-four years old, and I felt ancient.

Dean was gone. Just like my parents. Like my aunt. Like every foster family that promised forever, they delivered maybe a year's worth of care. Like every friend who was unable to handle the strangeness of being close to me.

I was alone. Again. Just like back then. Always.

But this time, it wasn't just me I had to worry about. I had an entire city depending on me. A city full of humans and Kin who did not know that their fate rested in the hands of a girl who couldn't even keep the people she loved from leaving her.

I couldn't bear the silence of my apartment anymore. Without really thinking about it, I walked, and then ran through the neon-lit streets of Vegas. My feet carried me to the only place that had always felt like home.

The cat cafe.

It was late, well past closing time, but my key still worked. I let myself in, the familiar smell of coffee and cat fur wrapping around me like a comforting blanket. In the dim light, I could make out the shapes of cat trees and cozy nooks.

I slumped into one of the oversized armchairs, my body finally giving in to the exhaustion. As if sensing my distress, a warm weight suddenly landed in my lap. I looked down to see Chili, the ginger tom, his creamsicle-colored fur glowing softly in the faint light from the street.

He meowed softly, bumping his head against my hand. Almost on autopilot, I stroked his fur, feeling the rumble of his purr against my legs.

"Oh, Chili," I whispered, my voice cracking. "What am I going to do?"

Chili, of course, didn't answer. He just purred louder, kneading my leg with his paws as if to say, "It's okay. I'm here."

And for a moment, just a moment, I didn't feel so alone.

I don't know how long I sat there, petting Chili and letting the tears fall. The neon lights of Vegas blinked through the windows, a reminder of the city I now had to protect. Dean's words echoed in my mind. *You're strong, Tam. Stronger than you know.*

I took a deep breath and brought myself back to the present. Back to the water-soaked office I stood in the middle of.

I had to be what Dean said I could be. Because right now, in this moment of gut-wrenching grief, I realized a terrible truth: in this position, with this responsibility, I would always end up alone.

The City had chosen me. And now, more than ever, I had to choose it back.

I stepped over the shattered remains of my office door. Remnants of its splintered husk lay scattered across the waiting area and within my office proper. Other than being soaked by the fire control system, everything seemed serviceable. My electronics were going to be toast. I groaned internally at the thought of what might have to be replaced but was also thankful for Malik's insistence on housing the City technology within the Library. The files were elsewhere, at least.

Part of me wondered if Elegast knew that.

Would he have stooped so far as to destroy City records on top of everything else?

Nothing would surprise me where he was concerned.

I made my way to my desk and paused. I stared at the desk. The cherry wood desk I had inherited from August Murr.

Bespoke Scully and Scully leather topped partner's desk ... Malik's voice echoed in my head. He had been so concerned about my leaving a ring on the surface from a beer bottle. Now the whole of it was soaked. My heart ached to see it.

Quincey could fix it.

The ache in my heart only intensified at the thought of dragging the DaVinci Crew in here to clean up this mess.

Elegast's mess.

Again.

I stared at the desk for a long time, just drinking in its familiarity. The carved designs, the years of buildup on its surface, the comfort of its presence. It was as much a part of me as I was a part of it.

No, I couldn't ask Quincey to fix it. This was a remnant of the past. Something I was holding on to because

I thought I needed to. I could replace it. And I would. But it wouldn't be the same.

Maybe that was ok?

I shook my head. I needed to think. I needed to plan… to cope. I needed to get to work. I needed to deal with Malik's fuck up and Elegast's actions and try to push back the sense of impending doom. I took a deep breath and started trudging through the dregs of my office. The water was ankle-deep on the hardwood floors and had soaked into the faux-suede chairs and couch.

This was going to be a nightmare of an insurance claim.

"It's an opportunity, Tam."

I felt the voice rather than heard it. I couldn't tell you whose voice it was or where it came from. It was familiar and foreign at the same time. It caught me off guard enough to make me stop and look around.

"Is someone here?" I called out.

There was no answer.

"Now I'm losing my damned mind on top of every-thing else," I muttered to myself. I pulled the top drawer open and fished around inside to recover a set of keys. They opened the doors to several City-owned shops and offices across the area. Half a dozen keys, silver and brass, dangled on a stereotypical Vegas souvenir keychain. A red and white poker chip with "Welcome to Las Vegas" printed on one side and "Make your own luck" on the other.

My eyes locked on the words pressed into the colorful charm.

Take a chance.

Roll the dice.

I shoved the keys into my pocket and walked outside.

I strode out of the Convention Center, my mind racing. The poker chip keychain felt heavy in my pocket, a reminder of the city I was sworn to protect. As I stepped onto the bustling street, the neon lights of Vegas, which always seemed to be on, pulsed with an urgent energy, mirroring my own frantic thoughts.

"Make your own luck," I muttered, fingering the keychain. Then it hit me. If I couldn't use the traditional channels, maybe it was time to create my own. These fuckers were stuck in loops and stories and patterns created for them centuries ago. But that wasn't me, that wasn't Vegas. The thought was terrifying and exhilarating all at once.

I pulled out my phone and scrolled through my contacts. My finger hovered over a name. Ambroginio D'Angelo. The ancient Blood-Kin who seemed to have his fingers in every pie in the city. Calling him was a risk. He would want something in return, something possibly dangerous. But desperate times called for desperate measures.

Taking a deep breath, I hit dial. As the phone rang, I scanned the street. A few passersby gave me curious looks, probably wondering why the Shard Keeper was standing on a street corner looking like she'd just survived a flood. In a way, I had.

"Ambroginio? It's Tamara. I have a proposition for you."

"Ah, Shard Keeper," Ambroginio's smooth voice answered, a hint of amusement coloring his tone. "I heard about the unfortunate situation with your offices."

Of course, he did. Someone who had him on speed dial no doubt sent him a note as soon as it all happened.

I squared my shoulders, feeling the weight of the city on them. Fine. Let's just do this. "I'm up against a clock and I need a host for some... disagreeing parties?"

"Mmmm, yes. That same situation we discussed earlier. A shame the only neutral area in the City was just desecrated by your Librarian," he quipped. "Oh, excuse me... former Librarian."

Dammit.

"He wasn't the only one involved, Ambroginio."

A pause.

"True."

My mind spun as I tried to regain control of the narrative.

"You and Malik are close, if I recall?" I asked.

"Perhaps," he evaded the question.

I tried to remember what Dean had told me about Banishment and Kin.

The only safe place for them is the established neutral ground. Which, if it was destroyed, means there is no safe place for them in the City. No territory they can go to with without risking war.

Who determines that area?

I do.

"Plazma is neutral ground, yes?"

"For my people, yes. I can't have them tearing into each other like rabid animals. We have the shifters for that, after all," he quipped.

"What if I named it neutral for everyone?"

There was a pause on the other end. I could almost hear the wheels turning in Ambroginio's ancient mind.

"Intriguing," he finally said. "Do go on."

"It doesn't have to be forever. Just until this situation is resolved. Then Malik would have some place to go..."

"Tempting. I confess. But I also sense there is another shoe hovering in the ether, waiting to drop. I doubt you called me to make such a magnanimous offer just to save the skin of your Librarian. So tell me, Keeper ... what...do...you...want?"

My heart pounded in my chest. This could go very wrong, quickly.

"I need a place where Oberon and Tatiyana can meet without tearing the city apart. Where I can try to broker a peace."

"And what makes you think I'd want to get involved in Fae politics, my dear?" Ambroginio's voice was silky smooth, but I could hear the underlying caution.

"Because you're trapped here," I said bluntly. "And this conflict could very well destroy the city you're bound to. Help me, and I'll owe you a favor. A big one."

I could almost hear the smile that spread over Ambroginio's face through the phone.

"Very well," Ambroginio said after I'd finished. His voice had lost its earlier amusement, replaced by a cold, calculated tone that sent shivers down my spine. "You have yourself a deal, Shard Keeper. But let's be clear about what you're asking."

I swallowed hard.

"You're not just asking for a venue, my dear. You're asking me to put my neck and my Kinship's territory on the line. We might make an enemy of whichever side feels slighted by the outcome." He paused, letting the weight of his words sink in. "That kind of risk doesn't come cheap."

"Name your price," I said, trying to keep my voice steady.

Ambroginio chuckled, a sound devoid of any warmth. "Oh, not yet. I think I'll hold on to this favor for a while. But when I call it in - and I will call it in - you'll answer. No questions asked. No matter what I ask. Are we clear?"

My mouth went dry. This was dangerous territory. Giving a Blood-Kin carte blanche was practically suicide. But what choice did I have?

"We're clear," I said.

"Excellent," Ambroginio purred. " When is it needed?"

I stopped and thought. The deal needed to be done by MidSummer. That was still a week away. But did I dare give Elegast more time to undermine the City? I couldn't. It was a risk I could not take.

"Tomorrow night."

I expected a pause, but none came. His response was swift and clear. "Then we have an accord. I'll see you then, Shard Keeper. And try to keep the warring children from destroying my club. Blood is such a pain to get out of the upholstery."

The line went dead, leaving me standing on the street corner, the full weight of what I'd just done crashing down on me. I looked up at the Vegas skyline, the Stratosphere Tower looming in the distance, a reminder of the heights we could reach—and how far we could fall.

"Well, City," I muttered, my voice barely above a whisper. "Looks like we're all in."

The New Librarian

The Library felt different as I descended the hidden staircase. Colder. More sterile. Malik's absence was palpable, his warmth and knowledge no longer permeating the air. Each step felt like a betrayal. Beto's words echoing in my mind: "We call for the removal of Malik Shah from his position as Librarian."

Banished. The word hung in my head like a crooked painting, always slightly off no matter how many times you adjust it.

Amrita was waiting for me in the main chamber, her white silk suit a stark contrast to the dark wood and leather-bound books surrounding us. Her steel-gray hair was pulled back in a severe bun, her dark eyes watching me intently.

Didn't even wait for the final vote, and she already moved in.

"Shard Keeper," she said, her voice neutral. "Thank you for coming."

I nodded, not trusting myself to speak. The betrayal of her seconding Malik's removal still stung.

"I understand your hesitation," Amrita continued, gesturing for me to take a seat. "But we have a city to protect, regardless of our personal feelings."

"The vote…"

"Will be what it will be. Whether Malik Shah retains his position, he destroyed neutral ground and must be banished. For how long will be a matter for debate and negotiation. Those negotiations could take hours or years. In the meantime, the City must not be without a Librarian."

"So you are here," I replied.

She nodded. "So I am here." She gestured to a chair. "Please."

As I sat, Amrita reached into her pocket and pulled out a small, intricately carved wooden box. "Before we begin, a gift. From one protector of knowledge to another."

I accepted the box with hesitation. Was this another ceremony I had not been taught? Was I expected to return something in exchange? I sighed and opened the box. Inside, I found a delicate silver pendant. Its design was abstract, reminding me somehow of both a key and a flame.

"It's beautiful," I said. "But why...?"

"Consider it a reminder," Amrita replied. "Of the power of knowledge, and of the responsibility we both bear. The key to unlock wisdom, and the flame to light the way. Both are needed to guide a city through dark times."

As I fastened the pendant around my neck, I felt a subtle warmth spread through me. Whether it was magic or simply the weight of Amrita's words, I couldn't say.

"Now," Amrita said, her tone shifting to business-like, "let's discuss the role of the Librarian. I suspect you have questions."

I nodded, curiosity overriding my lingering resentment. "What exactly does being the Librarian entail? I mean, I know Malik did a lot, and he told me some of it, but..."

Amrita's lips quirked into a small smile. "It's a complex role, Miss Hunter. Allow me to explain."

With a wave of her hand, shimmering glyphs appeared in the air between us. "Foremost, we are the keepers of knowledge. Every tome in this Library, every scroll, every artifact–they are our charge. We protect them, catalog them, and most importantly, we understand them."

I nodded as I followed along. Most of this was stuff that Malik had already told me. I gestured with my chin toward a bank of servers in the back of the room. Their lights flickered on and off in patterns only they understood.

"Mal said he digitized many of these?"

The edges of Amrit's mouth turned downward slightly. "Mmm. Yes. Well. I will have to deal with that at some point." Her displeasure was present for less than a moment before the practiced veneer returned to her face.

"You disapprove?"

Before answering, Amrita paused and said, "Shah and I disagreed on our opinions regarding modern record-keeping."

I nodded and remained silent.

The glyph morphed into a bridge. "We serve as a connection between the past and the present, between different factions of Kin, and between the supernatural world and the Shard Keeper." Her eyes met mine pointedly. "We are advisors, but we are not decision-makers. That burden falls on you."

Another glyph formed, this one a perfect circle. "We must remain neutral in Kin politics. It's a delicate balance, providing information without influencing outcomes."

"You don't feel that Malik was a neutral party to things, do you?" I asked.

She paused once more. It was a measured pause, as she clearly considered her reply. "Malik Shah was and is a product of the cities he has served. He has seen more centuries than any Hex-Kin ever has. I am certain his opinions were formed because of these experiences. Nonetheless-" Her eyes met mine. "-our personal opinions on the actions of other Kin must never impact our work. Ever."

"And the magic?" I asked. "Malik could do things I've never seen before."

Amrita's lips twitched. "Ah, yes. The magic." The glyphs swirled together, forming a complex, runic pattern. "As I mentioned, Malik Shah is an outlier among our people. No doubt his years of life and study have allowed him insights into magics others do not possess. Hex-Kin have a... unique relationship with magical energies. We can access and manipulate them in ways other Kin cannot. But..." her expression grew serious. "It comes at a cost. Every spell cast, every piece of hidden lore accessed — it takes something from us. A memory, a year of life, a piece of our very essence."

I felt a chill run down my spine. "That's why Malik seemed so... old sometimes. Even though he looked young."

Amrita nodded solemnly. "Indeed. It is the burden we bear as guardians of magical knowledge."

"Wait," I said, a thought striking me. "If accessing the knowledge is so costly, how do you share it with me without... you know, shriveling up or something?"

To my surprise, Amrita smiled. "That is where the pendant comes in. It's not just a symbol. It's a conduit. Through it, we can share knowledge more freely, more safely. Your connection to the city, to the very soul of Las Vegas, offsets the cost."

I frowned, my hand instinctively going to the pendant. "Malik never gave me anything like this. We worked together for years, and he never mentioned a pendant or a conduit."

Amrita's expression shifted, a mix of surprise and concern crossing her face. "The pendant is a tradition as old as the roles of Librarian and Shard Keeper themselves. Perhaps it is something unique to himself."

A nagging thought resurfaced in my mind. "Amrita," I began hesitantly, "what exactly happened in Xativa?"

The change in her demeanor was immediate. She sighed. "I suppose you have a right to know. It's a dark chapter in our history."

Amrita moved to a nearby shelf, her fingers trailing over the spines of the few books still there. "In 1707, Xativa was a thriving city in Spain, known for its paper production and its strategic importance. The Librarian there was... well, let's say he had grown complacent in his duties."

She turned back to me, her expression grave. "There was to be a dinner with visiting Kin dignitaries. It was the Librarian's duty to ensure all was prepared, to check for any potential issues. But he failed in this task."

I felt a chill run down my spine, sensing where this was going. "What happened?"

"During the dinner ceremonies, the City Shard fell ill," Amrita continued, her voice barely above a whisper. "An apparent allergy to pistachios - a common ingredient in the foods of the visiting dignitaries. But it was no accident."

My eyes widened. "It was deliberate?"

Amrita nodded solemnly. "The action was taken to weaken the strength of the City. You see, this was during the War of Spanish Succession. With the City's protections weakened, human forces were able to route Xativa. They burned it to the ground, Tamara. Massacred the inhabitants."

I felt sick. The idea that a Librarian's negligence could lead to such devastation... "And the Librarian?"

"Stripped of his position," Amrita said. "He found few places that would offer him refuge in Europe. No city would trust him after such a catastrophic failure."

Suddenly, a piece clicked into place. "Malik," I breathed. "It was Malik, wasn't it?"

Amrita's silence was answer enough.

"That's why he came to America," I realized. "There was nowhere in Europe that would have him."

"Yes," Amrita confirmed. " He traveled up and down the Eastern Seaboard of America for a while, staying where he could until the rumors of his background caught up with him and forced him to move. He finally came West with the railway and the settlers. Las Vegas, a young city with no established supernatural presence, was one of the few places where he could find a second chance."

I sank into a nearby chair, my mind reeling. Suddenly, so many of Malik's actions, his caution, his dedication - it all made sense. He'd been trying to atone for a mistake that cost thousands of lives.

"Why didn't he ever tell me?" I asked, more to myself than to Amrita.

Amrita's hand came to rest on my shoulder, a gesture of comfort. "Shame is a powerful force, Tamara. And some wounds never fully heal. Perhaps he thought he was protecting you by keeping his past hidden."

I nodded, still processing this revelation. It didn't excuse Malik's recent actions, but it certainly put them in a new light.

"Thank you for telling me," I said finally, looking up at Amrita. "I think... I think I understand him a little better now."

Amrita's smile was sad but understanding. "Understanding our past helps us shape our future. Now, shall we get back to the task at hand? We have a city to protect, after all." She turned back to her glyphs.

"I'm naming Plazma neutral ground," I blurted.

She froze. Her head tilted ever-so-slightly.

"Excuse me?" She turned back to face me.

"Elegast was clearly trying to make a power move by eliminating the only neutral space in the City... hoping I would fold, or allow him to pick the location." I reached up and rubbed the back of my neck.

Dammit Dean, why'd you have to be dead?

She nodded slowly. "Traditionally one allows the Kinship the ability to put foreward suggestions on a new location..."

"Ya, well, according to Dean, tradition would have also had a descendant of a Founding Family serving as Shard Keeper ... and you have me." I shrugged. "Clearly, the City feels tradition can get fucked."

She blinked quickly. It was the only sign that my words caught her off guard. "Blunt. But perhaps accurate. I'm sure Ambroginio is thrilled at the notion."

"Ambroginio will be paid for his services, which will aid the City ... and give Malik some place to hang his hat until all of this settles."

Amrita's mouth twitched upward slightly. "Clever."

"I'd like to think I am not a complete idiot." I looked around the room. In typical librarian fashion, there was not a hint of liquid anywhere in the room. I needed a drink.

"And if we survive this nonsense, I have another location in mind."

This time Amrita crossed her arms and shrugged. "Please tell me."

"How do you feel about cats and coffee?"

Treehouse Secrets

The text came just after midnight: "Container Park. 30 minutes. Come alone."

No signature, but I knew who it was from. My heart raced as I slipped out of my apartment, the neon-lit streets of Vegas a blur as I made my way downtown. The city never truly slept, but there was a distinct energy to it at this hour—a palpable sense of possibility and danger that hung in the air like the lingering scent of cigarette smoke and cheap perfume.

As I walked, the iconic Las Vegas skyline loomed above me, a glittering testament to human ambition and excess. The Stratosphere Tower pierced the night sky, its needle-like silhouette a beacon in the darkness. The Luxor's sky beam cut through the air, a pillar of light visible for miles around. And everywhere, the constant flickering of neon signs and LED displays created a kaleidoscope of color that danced across the faces of late-night revelers and weary service workers alike.

The pendant Amrita had given me earlier felt warm against my skin, a constant reminder of the weight of my responsibilities. I wondered, not for the first time, how many of the people I passed on the street knew about the hidden world that existed alongside their own. How many of them could sense the undercurrents of power that flowed through the city like an invisible river?

Container Park was a stark contrast to the gaudy excess of the Strip. Nestled in the heart of downtown, it was a more subdued affair–a collection of repurposed shipping containers transformed into boutique shops and eateries. During the day, it was a hub of local culture and commerce. But now, in the dead of night, it was eerily quiet, the usually bustling outdoor mall deserted.

The giant praying mantis sculpture at the entrance loomed over me, its metal limbs frozen mid-motion. In the daytime, it was a whimsical attraction, shooting flames from its antennae to the delight of tourists. Now, bathed in the ethereal glow of strategically placed spotlights, it looked almost menacing–a silent sentinel guarding secrets I was only beginning to understand.

I suppressed a shiver as I walked past it, heading for the children's treehouse in the center of the park. The recycled wood structure, typically alive with the laughter of kids, now stood silent and shadowy. It was the perfect place for a clandestine meeting–hidden in plain sight, yet easily overlooked.

A figure emerged from the shadows, and I tensed before recognizing the familiar silhouette.

"Malik," I breathed, relief and anxiety warring in my chest.

He looked different–tired, with dark circles under his eyes and a day's worth of stubble on his chin. But his amber eyes were as sharp as ever as they met mine, reflecting the distant neon glow that seemed to permeate every corner of the city.

"Tam," he said. "Thanks for coming."

"Are you okay?" I asked, unable to keep the concern from my voice despite everything that had happened. "Should you even be here? If they catch you—"

Malik's eyes darted around nervously. "I know the risks, Tam. Banishment isn't just about losing a job. It's... it's like being cut off from a part of yourself." He rubbed his chest absently, as if feeling a phantom pain. "The Library, the knowledge, the connection to the city's history–it's all gone. And if they catch me interfering..."

He didn't finish the thought, but he didn't need to. I knew the stories. Librarians who violated the terms of their banishment didn't just disappear–they were erased. From history, from memory, from existence itself.

"We shouldn't be doing this," I said, the reality of the situation hitting me. "Malik, if they find out—"

"Then they find out," he said firmly. "This is bigger than me, Tam. Bigger than both of us."

I nodded, swallowing hard. He was right, of course, but that didn't make it any easier. "So what now? We can't exactly waltz back into the Library."

Malik's lips quirked in a humorless smile. "No, we can't. I'm sure Amrita would just LOVE for me to try." He scowled and shook his head, then looked back at me. "I didn't come empty-handed, though." He patted his jacket pocket. "I managed to... liberate a few key documents before Amrita showed up and changed the locks... so to speak."

"Do you think she's involved?" I asked.

"I think the Kinship are motivated by power, and being Librarian is a powerful job," he replied. His shoulders rose and fell in a silent shrug. "I am not a popular man among the Kin."

"So I have been told."

He paused then and just stared at me. Centuries of unspoken pain in his eyes. It remained unspoken.

"Maybe when this is all over, you will let me tell my side of things?" he asked.

I nodded. How could I not? Malik had been my only anchor in this shit-show after Dean died. I wasn't ready to throw him out just yet.

"You got it."

Malik nodded grimly. "Okay. Follow me." He gestured to the tree house.

Why not? Everything else in this city was weird. Why not seek haven from supernatural creatures in a children's treehouse? I sighed and followed him.

As we climbed into the treehouse, I could smell the lingering scent of wood chips and the faint, sweet aroma of the nearby dessert shop—scents that seemed incongruous with the gravity of our meeting.

Once inside, he pulled out a small device and switched it on. A low hum filled the air, barely audible over the distant thrum of the city.

"Signal jammer," he explained at my questioning look. "Can't be too careful."

He took a deep breath, then dove in. "What happened at the office was not unprovoked. I need you to know that."

"I'm listening."

"After our talk, I did some digging into Oberon's past. It goes back further than we thought, Tam. Much further."

"How far are we talking?"

"Try the 5th century. Maybe earlier."

I felt my eyes widen. "That's... that's impossible. The Fae didn't come to America until—"

"Who said anything about America?" Malik interrupted. "Oberon Elegast isn't just old, Tam. He's Old World. And he brought his Old World problems with him when he came here."

Malik pulled out a worn leather journal and handed it to me. The smell of aged paper and ink hit me, a contrast to the synthetic scents of the modern city around us. "This is a record of Fae migrations to the New World. Look at the entry for 1872."

I flipped through the pages until I found the date. There, in faded ink, was a list of names. My breath caught as I read one particular entry:

Oberon Elegast, accompanied by seven changelings (ages 3-12)

"Seven children," I whispered, the horror of it sinking in. The treehouse suddenly felt claustrophobic, the weight of centuries pressing down on us.

Malik nodded grimly. "And that's just one crossing. I've found evidence of similar patterns going back centuries. Oberon doesn't just take children, Tam. He collects them."

"But why?" I asked, my mind reeling. "The Fae need human children to sustain their numbers, sure, but this... this is something else."

"Power," Malik said simply. "Each child taken, each life transformed, it all feeds into his power. And the longer he does it..."

"The stronger he gets," I finished, feeling sick.

Malik nodded. "Exactly. And now he's set his sights on this latest child. If he gets his hands on it—"

"It won't just be about one kid," I realized. "It'll be about cementing his power base here in Vegas."

"Bingo."

We sat in silence for a moment, the weight of this revelation settling over us. Through the gaps in the treehouse walls, I could see slivers of the Vegas skyline—a glittering reminder of all that was at stake. My mind raced, connecting dots I hadn't even known existed. "Beto," I said suddenly. "Is he...?"

Malik's expression softened. "One of Oberon's collected children? Almost certainly. But Tam, you have to understand—Beto might not even know the full extent of his own history. The Fae are masters of manipulation, even of their own kind."

I thought of Beto's betrayal, of the conflict I'd seen in his eyes. Could this explain his actions? Was he as much a victim in all this as the child we were trying to protect?

"What about Tatiyana?" I asked. "Does she know about all this?"

Malik shrugged. "It's hard to say. The Fae courts are labyrinthine at the best of times. The records show that they have not had an increase in population for some time. This tithe may have been Oberon's first real chance since the two of them split up. The first chance for him to stake a claim entirely his own. She might fully know and oppose Oberon for that very reason. Or she might be an unwitting pawn in a game centuries in the making."

I rubbed my temples, feeling a headache coming on. "How the hell am I supposed to fight something like this?"

Malik reached out, his hand hovering near mine, before pulling back. "You're not alone in this, Tam. You have allies–me, Andy Mak, the DaVinci crew. Hell, even Ambroginio, in his own twisted way."

"But will it be enough?"

Malik's eyes met mine, and I saw a fierce determination there. "It has to be. For the sake of the child, for Vegas, for all the children Oberon has taken over the centuries–it has to be enough."

Finally, I asked the question that had been nagging at me since I got his text. "Why are you telling me this, Malik? Why risk everything to help me after... after what happened?"

Malik's eyes met mine, and I saw a depth of emotion there that made my chest ache. "Because it's the right thing to do," he replied. "Because this city needs you, Tam. And because..." he hesitated, then pushed on, "because you're my friend. No matter what."

I felt tears prick at the corners of my eyes. "Malik, I—"

He held up a hand, stopping me. "Don't. We don't have time for apologies or explanations. Just... use this information. Stop Oberon. Save the kid."

I nodded, swallowing hard. "I will. I promise."

As we prepared to leave, Malik caught my arm. "Be careful, Tam. Oberon's had centuries to perfect his game. He won't go down easy."

"I know," I said. "But neither will I."

Malik's expression turned serious. "There's something else you need to understand. By helping you, I've violated the terms of my banishment. If the Kinship finds out..."

I nodded. The weight of the pendant Amrita had given me suddenly felt heavier against my chest. "I know. But there's something else you should know. I've made a deal with Ambroginio D'Angelo."

Malik's eyebrows shot up. "Ambroginio? Tam, that's dangerous territory."

"I know, I know. But we needed a neutral ground for negotiations, and Plazma was the best option." I took a deep breath. "It's been officially declared neutral territory for the duration of this crisis."

Malik whistled low. "That's... actually quite clever. Risky, but clever. Oberon is not gonna expect that."

"Yeah, well, desperate times and all that." I met his eyes, my voice softening. "Listen, if you need a safe place, go to Plazma. Ambroginio knows the score, and he'll honor the neutrality agreement. It's not much, but it's something."

For a moment, I saw a flicker of the old Malik - the one who had guided me through my early days as Shard Keeper. His eyes warmed with gratitude. "Thank you, Tam. That... that means more than you know." He paused a moment, wrestling with words that needed to be said. "You need to be prepared for what it might mean. If I disappear—"

"Don't," I cut him off, not wanting to hear it.

"If I disappear," he continued, undeterred, "everything we've discussed, everything I've shown you—it might disappear too. The Kinship has ways of... editing reality. You'll need to hold on to this information, Tam. No matter what happens to me."

The weight of his words settled over me like a heavy cloak. I nodded, my throat tight. "I understand."

"Good," Malik said softly. "Now go. And Tam? Whatever happens... it's been an honor."

We parted ways outside the park, Malik melting into the shadows while I headed back to the garish lights of the Strip. The contrast was jarring–from the quiet, conspiratorial atmosphere of our meeting to the never-ending party that was Las Vegas Boulevard.

As I walked, I felt the familiar weight of the city settling onto my shoulders. But now, added to that weight, was the burden of secrecy, of forbidden knowledge, and the genuine possibility that I might be the only one left to remember the truth. The neon lights seemed brighter somehow, the energy of the city more vibrant. It was as if Vegas itself was rallying to the cause, lending me its strength.

I had information now. I had a plan forming. And most importantly, I knew I wasn't alone in this fight–even if that support came at a terrible risk.

My hand went to the pendant around my neck, feeling its comforting warmth. The key to unlock wisdom, and the flame to light the way. Well, I had the wisdom now. It was time to light the way forward.

Can I trust you, Amrita? Maybe not just yet.

I pulled out my phone and dialed a number, the blue glow of the screen illuminating my face in the neon-tinged night.

"Nicky? It's Tam."

Resistence

I was brought into the world at the exact time that the moon was in the darkest shadow of a lunar eclipse and closest to the Heart of the Earth. It sounded like the beginning to a good fantasy story, but superstitions and metaphysical beliefs existed for a reason. There were things that existed in our world that science could not explain.

There really were no words to describe what it was like to carry around the spirit-being of an entire City. It wasn't like I was in constant communication with some otherworldly entity that was whispering secrets and desires in the back of my mind. It also wasn't like I would lose control of my body while some spirit possessed me and walked around the Vegas Strip.

Early Shard history talked about areas where the Kinship would keep their Shard in a secure location, like a prized pet. While that helped to keep the City safe and secure, it also resulted in the residents of the city developing xenophobia and wide-scale depression. In some other locations, the Shard was treated almost like royalty, dictating territories and allotting options to whatever Kin earned their favor.

Malik had mentioned that the Blood-Kin would never think to poison me, because my health affected the health of others, and that was true. As an example, if I stepped on a nail and contracted a blood infection like tetanus, suddenly the blood supply of the City might also contract an infection. That tie went both ways, though. If there were a significant break in the sewer lines that affected several city blocks, I would end up worshiping the porcelain throne.

Tatiyana had taken a huge chance when she launched that ball of electricity at me. The scar would heal, but it also meant that some area of the cityscape was going to undergo a change in appearance because of the damage caused. Malik's magic had ensured the damage would be small. If she'd caused me to have a heart attack... well, let's just say that the blackout of 2004 had resulted in August Murr changing his diet.

Because of that cause and effect relationship, many Shards managed a carefully curated balance of independence and watchful Kinship keeping. Older Shards had generations to work out roles and responsibilities. There were rules and mandates set into place for centuries.

We didn't have that here.

Maybe it was because America was so young. Or maybe it was because the colonists that came here rejected the Old World ideals that still governed many Shards and their Kin. Maybe it was because of the underworld influence of Bugsy Malone, prohibition, smuggling, gambling and the host of other illegal activities that the City was known for that flavored how things were done here. I couldn't explain it, but it was part of who I was now. All I knew was there was always an element of something hidden in every transaction. It made trusting one another challenging at best.

It made what I was about to do even harder.

The early morning sun cast long shadows across the industrial park as I approached DaVinci's. I wanted sleep. I wanted a sandwich. And most of all, I just wanted this to be over.

The makerspace looked different in the harsh light of day—less a sanctuary of creativity and more a fortress bracing for impact. Or maybe that was just my perspective, colored by the weight of what I was about to ask.

I paused at the entrance, my hand hovering over the door handle. The last time I was here, Nicky had made it clear she wanted nothing to do with Fae business. Now I was about to drag them all back into the thick of it.

I'd be lucky if she didn't hit me with a wrench.

Was I really doing this? A wave of doubt washing over me. Was I really going to risk their safety and their sanity for this fight? But then I remembered Malik's words, the centuries of stolen children, and I knew I had no choice. The alternative was unthinkable.

Taking a deep breath, I pushed the door open. The familiar scents of sawdust, machine oil, and soldering flux hit me like a wall. For a moment, I was transported back to simpler times—high school shop classes, late-night tinkering sessions, dreams untainted by supernatural politics. A pang of nostalgia mixed with regret shot through me.

"Well, look what the cat dragged in," a voice called out. Tom emerged from behind a half-assembled motorcycle, wiping his hands on a rag. His eyes, so similar to Nicky's, were wary as they met mine.

"Hey, Tom," I said, trying for a casual tone and failing miserably. My heart was pounding, and I felt like an imposter.

They can probably see right through me.

"Is Nicky around?"

He jerked his head towards the back of the shop. "Office. But I wouldn't—"

I was already moving past him. "Thanks."

As I walked through the workshop, I couldn't help but notice the sidelong glances from the other makers. They knew who I was, what I represented. The air felt thick with unspoken tension.

The guilt was almost overwhelming.

I found Nicky hunched over a drafting table, her blonde mohawk a sharp distinction to the precise lines of the blueprint before her. She didn't look up as I entered.

"I told you I was out, Tam," she said, her voice tight. "Was my hanging up on you an hour ago unclear?"

I winced. Her words stung, but I couldn't blame her. How many times have I put them in danger? I wondered. How many times have I asked too much?

"I know. And I wouldn't be here if it wasn't important. Life-or-death important."

That got her attention. She looked up, her blue eyes searching my face. Whatever she saw there made her sigh heavily. "Shit. Alright, let's hear it."

I perched on the edge of her desk, gathering my thoughts. How do you explain centuries of child abduction and magical power plays in a way that doesn't sound completely insane?

She's going to think I've lost it, I thought. Hell, maybe I have.

"It's about Oberon," I started. "And the child he's trying to claim."

Nicky's face hardened. "Of course it is. When isn't it about that bastard?"

"This is different," I pressed on, trying to keep the desperation out of my voice. "It's bigger than just one kid. Oberon... he's been doing this for centuries, Nick. Stealing children, turning them into changelings. And each time he does it, he gets stronger."

I laid out everything Malik had told me—the journal entries, the pattern of abductions stretching back to the 5th century, the implications for Vegas if Oberon claimed this latest child. As I spoke, I saw the color drain from Nicky's face. My stomach churned. I'm asking her to face her worst nightmare, I realized. Again.

"Jesus Christ," she whispered when I finished. "And Beto? Is he...?"

I nodded grimly. "Almost certainly one of Oberon's 'collected' children. He might not even know the full extent of it."

The thought of Beto—my Beto—being one of Oberon's victims made my heart ache. How much of what we had was real? I wondered. How much was shaped by Oberon's machinations?

Nicky stood abruptly, pacing the small office. "This is... fuck, Tam. This is huge. But what do you expect us to do about it? We're not exactly equipped to take on an ancient Fae lord."

"No," I agreed, feeling the weight of our limitations. "But you are equipped to help me set up a neutral ground for negotiations on short order. And maybe... maybe find a loophole in Fae contract law."

She stopped pacing, staring at me incredulously. "A loophole? In Fae law? Are you out of your mind?"

Probably, I thought. But what choice do we have?

"Probably," I admitted aloud. "But it's our best shot at stopping this without all-out war. I spoke with Amrita—the new Librarian—about it all."

Nicky's eyes narrowed. "And you trust this Amrita? After what happened to Malik?"

I hesitated. The truth was, I didn't know if I could trust anyone anymore. Every alliance felt fragile, every friendship tainted by the possibility of betrayal. "I... I don't know if I trust her. But I trust she wants to protect the city. And right now, our interests align."

It wasn't a complete lie. Amrita had been very up-front about her role and what she knew about Malik. When I asked her about the situation with Oberon, she, like Malik, pointed me to the debt that Nicky held. They both thought that Nicky Botham was the solution. Though I still couldn't see how.

"Tam..." Nicky's voice was soft, almost pitying. "You know how this ends. The Fae always win. They always get what they want."

Her words hit me like a physical blow. Because part of me believed them. Part of me was terrified that we were already doomed, that all of this was just delaying the inevitable. But I couldn't let that fear win. I couldn't let Oberon win.

"Not this time," I said, my voice firmer than I felt. "Not if we can help it. Nick, I know I'm asking a lot. I know you have every reason to say no. And your reasons are valid. But this isn't just about us anymore. It's about every kid in Vegas. Hell, it's about every kid Oberon might set his sights on in the future. You once told me that when the Fae screwed with your head, you felt like you'd lost a piece of yourself. That you'd never be whole again."

Nicky flinched, and I hated myself a little for bringing up those painful memories. But I had to make her understand.

"Help me, Nick. Help me stop Oberon from tearing any more kids apart."

For a long moment, the silence stretched between us, heavy with unspoken fears and shared history. Please, I thought desperately. Please understand. Please help.

Then, slowly, she reached out and placed her hand on my shoulder. I saw a flicker of... something... in her eyes.

Determination? Hope? I couldn't be sure. But it felt like a lifeline in a storm.

"I must be out of my damn mind," she muttered. Then, louder, "Alright. I'm in. But I'm not speaking for the others. You want their help, you ask them yourself."

Relief washed over me so strongly I felt dizzy. It wasn't a full victory, but it was a start. "Thank you," I said, meaning it with every fiber of my being.

Nicky nodded, then called out, "Tom! Quincey! Cozy! Get your asses in here! We've got a situation to discuss."

As the others filed in, looking equal parts curious and apprehensive, I steeled myself for another round of explanations and persuasion. My throat felt dry, my palms sweaty. What if they say no? What if this is too much to ask?

But as I looked at the faces of my friends–people who'd been through hell because of the Fae and come out the other side–I felt a spark of hope. They were survivors, all of them. And maybe, just maybe, that's exactly what we needed to be to win this fight.

We can do this, I told myself, trying to believe it. *We have to do this.*

Time to roll the dice and see where they land.

It was a warm evening, about a month after I'd accepted the role of Shard Keeper. Dean and I were sitting on the roof of the Fremont Street Experience, our legs dangling over the edge as we watched the light show below. Apparently, being Shard Keeper meant I could gain access to areas of the City I never could before. Go figure. Below us, Vegas pulsed with energy, a living, breathing entity that I was only beginning to understand.

"Close your eyes, Tam," Dean said.

I shot him a skeptical look but complied. The darkness behind my eyelids was soon filled with the afterimages of neon lights.

"Now, breathe deeply," Dean instructed. "Feel the air in your lungs. The concrete under your hands. The vibrations of the city all around you."

I took a deep breath, trying to focus on the sensations Dean described. At first, all I felt was the hard roof beneath me and the warm breeze on my skin.

"Good," Dean's voice came from beside me. "Now, reach out with your mind. Don't try to see the city. Try to feel it."

"Reach out with my mind... do you have any idea how ridiculous you sound?"

"Yes, I do."

I furrowed my brow. He was serious. "I don't know how—"

"Don't think," Dean interrupted gently. "Just feel. The city is alive, Tam. It has a heartbeat. Find it."

I took another deep breath, trying to quiet my doubts. I focused on the surrounding sounds–the music from the light show, the chatter of tourists, the distant hum of traffic. Gradually, these distinct noises blended into a single, pulsing rhythm.

And then I felt it.

It was like a current of electricity running through my body, connecting me to every light, every building, every person in Vegas. I could feel the hope of the gamblers, the weariness of the workers, the excitement of the newlyweds. The weight of the city's history pressed on me, along with the wild potential of its future.

"Oh," I breathed, my eyes flying open. "Oh, wow."

Dean was smiling at me, his eyes twinkling. "You felt it, didn't you?"

I nodded, still overwhelmed by the sensation. "Is it always like that?"

"It gets easier to tap into," Dean said. "But it never stops being amazing."

I looked out at the city with fresh eyes, seeing beyond the neon and glitter to the living entity beneath. "It's... it's beautiful," I murmured.

"It is," Dean agreed. "And now it's a part of you, Tam. Just as you're a part of it."

I turned to him, suddenly anxious. "What if I'm not strong enough? What if I can't handle it?"

Dean's expression softened. "The City chose you, Tam. It saw something in you it needed. Trust that."

"But how do I know what it needs?" I asked. "How do I make the right decisions?"

"Listen to it," Dean said simply. "The way you did just now. The city will guide you if you let it. It's not just about protecting buildings or people. It's about nurturing the soul of Vegas."

I nodded slowly, beginning to understand. "So when you say the city comes first..."

"I mean that this connection, this bond you're forming, it has to be your priority," Dean finished. "It doesn't mean you can't have relationships or a life of your own. But this—" he gestured at the sprawling cityscape before us, "—this has to be your true north."

I took another deep breath, feeling the pulse of the city thrumming through me. It was exhilarating and terrifying all at once. "I think I understand," I said.

Dean squeezed my shoulder. "You're going to make mistakes, Tam. You're going to struggle sometimes. But always come back to this feeling. Let the city guide you."

I nodded, a new sense of purpose filling me. "I will," I promised.

tête-à-tête

Without the pulsing neon and obscure clientele, Plaz-ma's true nature revealed itself. The sleek, modern design blended seamlessly with touches of old-world opulence — a perfect reflection of its owner and its new status as neutral ground for all.

The iconic neon sign of the dripping bottle was dark but still commanded attention. Inside, the space had been transformed. The dance floor, often populated with intimately entangled couples, was now cleared, creating an open space for negotiations. The private alcoves, typically hidden behind heavy velvet curtains, stood open, their plush interiors visible to all — a symbol of the transparency required for these delicate talks.

Crystalline chandeliers hung dormant, their facets catching the sunlight streaming through hidden skylights. The polished hardwood floor gleamed like honey. Along the walls, symbols of various Kin factions had been carefully placed, adding to the allure and mystery of the club.

The upstairs area, with its one-way glass overlooking the main floor, had been converted into observation galleries.

Most notably, the discrete phlebotomists that once provided blood-letting services were gone, replaced by neutral refreshment areas catering to the diverse needs of all Kin types. It was a simple message: in this space, all were equal, all were guests.

Ambroginio assured me that his people understood the need for this small and brief sacrifice. It would not be long before a more suitable location was chosen. Two weeks of inconvenience at best, he told them. After all, a City could not be without a meeting space. Certainly not a City the size of Las Vegas.

I wondered how much of that reassurance was the truth, and how much this would bite me in the ass later.

The air, free from the usual cocktail of perfumes, sweat, and desire, held the faintest trace of sandalwood and something metallic — blood, perhaps, or simply the lingering echo of countless nights of passion and hunger. But now, it was tinged with something else — anticipation, tension, and the faint crackle of power.

Plazma had always been a place where the supernatural world brushed against the mortal one. Now, as neutral ground, it stood as a bridge between warring factions, a delicate balance point in the precarious politics of the Kin. The weight of its new role was palpable, hanging in the air like the moment before a lightning strike.

As I stepped inside, I couldn't help but marvel at the transformation. Ambroginio had outdone himself. The question was, would it be enough to prevent an all-out war?

"Keeper!" Ambroginio's voice rang out as we entered, shattering the almost reverent silence. "You've brought friends! How delightful!"

The ancient Blood-Kin swept towards us, his appearance a study in contrasts. Gone was the casual resort wear, replaced by a suit that seemed to change colors as he moved — now emerald, now sapphire, now a deep garnet. The fabric shimmered like oil on water, catching the light in ways that shouldn't be possible. It was a theatrical, borderline gaudy, yet undeniably impressive — much like Plazma itself.

His thick black hair was meticulously styled, and his iconic mustache had been trimmed and waxed to perfection. Gold chains still glinted at his neck, each link probably worth more than most people made in a year. His fingers, still perfectly manicured, were adorned with rings that seemed to pulse with subtle power — magical protections, no doubt, befitting his role as neutral host.

But it was his eyes that caught my attention. Those dark orbs, sharp despite his flamboyant demeanor, took in every detail of the room and its occupants. The grandfatherly warmth was still there, but now it was tempered with something else — a keen awareness of the high-stakes game we were all playing.

"Welcome to Plazma," he said, spreading his arms wide in a gesture that was both welcoming and slightly mocking. "Neutral ground, as promised. A haven for all our... distinguished guests."

His voice, still deep and rich, carried an undercurrent of amusement, as if he found the whole situation terribly entertaining. But beneath that, I caught a hint of steel — a reminder that this was his domain, and he would brook no violation of its neutrality.

"Ambroginio," I nodded, trying to keep my voice neutral. "Thank you for agreeing to host."

"Oh, please," he waved a hand dismissively, gold rings catching the light. "As if I'd miss this show. Now, introduce me to your little entourage!"

I could feel the DaVinci crew tensing behind me. This was exactly what they'd been afraid of–the flamboyant unpredictability of the Kin world. Fae were one threat, but this? Ambroginio was a Blood-Kin aka a Vampire. Humanity's love of legends and lore did these Kin injustice in some respects. But in others, they were on the nose. It was hard to know where to draw the line on trust when one party was probably sizing the other up for lunch.

There was steel beneath Ambroginio's silky manner, a danger I couldn't afford to forget.

"This is Nicky, Tom, Quincey, and Cozy," I said, introducing each. "They're here to help set up."

Ambroginio clapped his hands together, the sound echoing in the cavernous space. "Marvelous! I do love a good makeover. Shall we start with the lighting? I'm thinking dramatic spotlights, very film noir..."

As Ambroginio led us deeper into the club, he kept up a running commentary, pointing out features with the pride of a peacock displaying its feathers. "That bar? Mahogany, imported from Brazil. The stools are upholstered in genuine leather from Italian cattle. And see that statue? Ancient Greek, or so they told me. Who knows if it's real ...well... I do, and it's not... but it certainly classes up the place, doesn't it?"

All the while, his eyes never stopped moving, cataloging every reaction, every micro-expression of his new guests. He was particularly fascinated by Nicky, sensing in her a strength and defiance that both attracted and challenged him.

"We're not here for aesthetics," Nicky cut in, her voice sharp. "We're here to help create a space that can withstand Fae manipulation."

Ambroginio's eyebrows shot up, a predatory grin spreading across his face. "My, my. Aren't you a feisty one?" He leaned in conspiratorially. "I like that in a woman."

I stepped between them, acutely aware of the thin ice we were treading on. "Ambroginio, we appreciate your hospitality. But this needs to be more than just a stage. We're trying to outmaneuver Oberon here."

At the mention of Oberon's name, something shifted in Ambroginio's eyes. The playful glint was replaced by something colder, more calculated. Centuries of politics and power plays flashed behind those ageless eyes.

"Ah, yes. Our dear Lord Elegast." Ambroginio's voice dropped an octave, all traces of camp vanishing. "Tell me, little Shard Keeper, do you really think you can beat him at his own game?"

I thought of Dean's lessons, of the City's pulse thrumming through me. "I have to try."

Ambroginio studied me for a long moment, then nodded. "Very well. Let's see what your little team can do." He looked at them all with more than casual judgment. "And remember, when all of this is done, it gets retro-fitted back."

For the next few hours, Plazma became a hive of activity. Quincey and Tom worked on reinforcing the physical structure, while Nicky and Cozy focused on more esoteric protections. I moved between them, coordinating efforts and trying to keep Ambroginio from being too... Ambroginio.

"No, no, no!" the Blood_kin cried, rushing over to where Cozy was setting up a circle of salt. "You can't use that generic table salt. Here, use this." He produced a container of pink Himalayan salt with a flourish. "Much more chic, and it has trace minerals. The Fae simply adore it."

Cozy looked at me helplessly. I shrugged. "Humor him," I mouthed.

As the day wore on, I could feel the tension building. This wasn't just about setting up a meeting space. We were preparing for a battle, one that would be fought with words and contracts rather than swords and spells, but no less deadly for it.

"Tam," Nicky called me over. She was frowning at a series of runes she'd drawn from the images she had been given. "Are you sure about these runes? I mean, I'm no mage..."

No, the one I trusted got himself banished, but those are the ones he said to use.

"Hex-Kin," I corrected, then quickly bit my tongue. The DaVinci crew all turned and looked at me.

It was the Shard training showing through. A month ago, I would have said the same thing. Now I felt obligated to use their proper terms. I held up my hands in apology.

"I'm sorry, you're here helping, and I'm criticizing your terms..."

Nicky shook her head, "Nope, it's fair. They deserve to be called what they choose to be called." She looked back at the sigils. "Shouldn't someone ... you know ... magically inclined ... be doing this?"

"They're decorative, my dear." Ambroginio offered. His eyes met mine, and he smiled. "They look close enough to make someone pause before taking action, but ..." he placed his right hand on his hip and gestured around the room with his left, "Do you honestly think I would allow random runes to be placed in Plazma without my consent? I have a clientele to think of." He winked at me.

I allowed myself a small smile. "Just remember our deal. You help us pull this off, and we'll free you from this place. Fairly and legally."

Ambroginio placed a hand over his heart. "Cross my heart and hope to die. Again."

As the day wore on and the preparations continued, Ambroginio found himself increasingly invested in the outcome. These humans, with their brief lives and burning intensity, had brought something new into his world. And while part of him still saw them as play-things, another part–a part he thought long dead–rooted for their success.

After all, eternal life could get so dreadfully boring without the occasional shake-up.

It was late afternoon when Ambroginio caught my arm, pulling me aside with a strength that belied his theatrically languid demeanor. His voice dropped to a purr. Meant for my ears alone.

"My dear Shard Keeper, while I'm absolutely thrilled by this little... renovation project you've brought to my humble abode, I do hope you haven't forgotten our own little tête-à-tête?"

I felt a chill run down my spine, remembering the weight of the debt I'd incurred. "I haven't forgotten, Ambroginio."

His smile widened, showing just a hint of fang. "Excellent. I'd hate for there to be any... misunderstandings between us. Especially with so much at stake."

I glanced at the DaVinci crew, busy with their preparations, blissfully unaware of the dangerous currents swirling just beneath the surface of our interaction.

"What exactly are you asking for?" I kept my voice low, matching his tone.

Ambroginio's eyes glittered with amusement and something darker. "Oh, nothing too onerous. Yet. Let's just say that when the time comes, I'll expect you to be...

flexible in your interpretation of certain rules. After all, we're both servants of this marvelous City, are we not? Sometimes, the greater good requires a little... moral flexibility."

The implication hung in the air between us, heavy with potential consequences. I thought of Dean's lessons, of the City's pulse beating in my veins. What would the greater good demand of me?

"I'll honor our deal," I said carefully. "But I won't compromise the safety of Vegas or its people."

Ambroginio threw his head back and laughed, the sound echoing off the club's high ceilings. "Oh, my dear, that's what I love about you, Shard Keeper. So earnest, so dedicated." His expression sobered, though his eyes still danced with mirth and danger. "Just remember, my dear — in this game we're playing, everyone has an angle. Even me. Especially me."

He patted my cheek in a gesture that was both affectionate and condescending. "Now, let's get back to our delightful guests, shall we? I believe the fierce little blonde one is about to attempt something spectacularly ill-advised with those wards, and I simply must see how it turns out."

As Ambroginio sauntered away, I felt the weight of my responsibilities settle even more heavily on my shoulders. The city, the DaVinci crew, the impending confrontation with Oberon, and now this reminder of my debt to Ambroginio–it was a precarious balance, and one misstep could send it all tumbling down.

Oberon might have centuries of experience and Fae magic on his side. But we had something he could never understand–the soul of Vegas itself. And I'll be damned if we would not use every trick in the book to make it count.

I knew the next step would be the hardest: informing Oberon Elegast and Tatiyana Scawen of the meeting. My hands trembled slightly as I reached for my phone.

I called Tatiyana first. As the wronged party, she deserved the courtesy of the first notification.

"Your Grace," I said when she answered, my voice steadier than I felt. "I've arranged a neutral meeting ground to discuss the matter of the changeling child."

There was a pause, then Tatiyana's cool voice came through. "Indeed? And where might this 'neutral ground' be, given recent... events?"

I took a deep breath. "Plazma. The Blood-Kin establishment. I've declared it neutral territory for the duration of our meeting."

Another pause. I could almost hear her weighing the implications.

"Interesting choice, Shard Keeper," she finally said. "Very well. When?"

I gave her the details, and she agreed without further comment. One down, one to go.

Calling Oberon was... harder. My finger hovered over his number for several seconds before I finally pressed 'call.' The phone rang once, twice, three times. Each ring felt like an eternity, the weight of what I was about to do pressing down on me.

"Well, well," his silky voice purred, sending an involuntary shiver down my spine. "To what do I owe this pleasure, little Shard Keeper?"

I steeled myself, gripping the phone tighter. "Lord Elegast. I'm calling to inform you of a meeting I've arranged. Regarding the changeling child."

His laugh was like ice cracking, cold and sharp. "Oh? And what makes you think I'd agree to such a meeting? The child is mine by right. There is nothing to discuss."

"Because," I said, channeling every ounce of authority I could muster, "as Shard Keeper, it's my duty to maintain balance in this city. This conflict threatens that balance. It threatens the very fabric of our community."

"Community?" Oberon scoffed. "You speak as if we are all equals, child. Have you forgotten who I am? What I am capable of?"

I closed my eyes, remembering the destruction of my office, the fear in Nicky's eyes, and the weight of the city's future on my shoulders. "I haven't forgotten, Your Grace. But perhaps you have forgotten the power of the Shard. This City chose me, and I will do whatever it takes to protect it."

The silence that followed was deafening. When Oberon spoke again, his voice had lost its amused edge. "You play a dangerous game, Tamara Lyn Hunter. Do you truly understand what you're risking? This isn't just about a child or a tithe. This is about the balance of power that has existed for centuries."

"I understand more than you think, Your Grace," I replied, surprised by the steadiness in my voice. "I understand that if this conflict continues, it could tear Vegas apart. I understand the consequences will affect not just the Fae, but every Kin in this city, and every human who calls it home."

"And you think you can prevent this?" Oberon's voice was quieter now, but no less dangerous. "You, a mere mortal, barely more than a child yourself?"

I thought of Dean, of his faith in me. Of Beto, and the love we shared. Of Nicky and the DaVinci crew, and all the ordinary people of Vegas who did not know the supernatural storm brewing around them.

"I have to try," I said simply. "Will you attend the meeting, Your Grace?"

The silence stretched so long that I thought he might have hung up. I could almost see him in my mind's eye, weighing his options, and calculating the risks and potential gains.

Finally, he spoke. "You play a dangerous game, child. But very well. I shall attend your little... gathering. But mark my words, Shard Keeper. If this is some ploy, some attempt to undermine my authority, the consequences will be... severe. Not just for you, but for every soul in this city you claim to protect."

The threat hung in the air, almost tangible in its intensity. I swallowed hard but kept my voice steady. "I understand, Your Grace. Thank you for your cooperation."

As I ended the call, I let out a shaky breath, my hands trembling. It was done. For better or worse, the wheels were in motion.

Parlay

As twilight descended upon Las Vegas, Plazma transformed. The club, once a playground for Blood-Kin desires, now stood as a nexus of supernatural power. The air thrummed with anticipation, each breath charged with the potential for both miracle and catastrophe.

I stood at the center of it all, the weight of the City pressing down on me. It was palpable. My palms were sweaty, and I could feel my heart racing. This was it. Everything I'd worked for, everything I'd sacrificed, it all came down to this moment.

Please don't let me fuck this up.

Ambroginio seemed to materialize at my side, now clad in an impeccably tailored suit in deep burgundy. This man's closet must have been endless.

"They're coming," he murmured, his dark eyes fixed on the entrance. "I can feel it in my bones. Well, what's left of them, anyway." He flashed me a grin that was equal parts charm and menace.

"Are we ready?" I asked, hating the tremor in my voice.

Ambroginio's expression softened for a moment. "As ready as we'll ever be, little Shard Keeper. Remember, in this game, the house doesn't always win... but it never loses everything."

Before I could ponder his cryptic words, the air outside Plazma began to shimmer and twist. Reality itself seemed to bend, folding back like a curtain to reveal a sight that took my breath away.

Tatiyana Scawen, the Laird of Las Vegas, stepped through the rift in space. She was resplendent in a gown that seemed woven from moonlight and shadow, each movement sending ripples of starlight cascading across the fabric. Her hair, once ink-black, now shone with streaks of silver that caught the light like polished blades. At her throat gleamed a pendant of black opal, swirling with colors that shouldn't exist in our reality.

Behind her came her retinue, each Fae more breathtaking and terrible than the last. Some bore the appearance of beautiful humans, while others embraced their otherworldly nature — eyes like gems, skin that shimmered with impossible hues, limbs that moved with a grace that defied physics.

Tatiyana's gaze swept the room, and when her eyes met mine, I felt a chill race down my spine. There was recognition there, and respect, but also a cold calculation that reminded me of just how alien these beings truly were.

"Shard Keeper," she intoned, her voice like distant thunder. "You have our gratitude for arranging this parley. May it prove... fruitful."

I inclined my head, careful to maintain eye contact. "Your Grace. Plazma stands ready to serve as neutral ground. May wisdom guide our words this night."

A smile flickered across her face, there and gone in an instant. "Indeed. Though I wonder, child, if you truly understand what you have set in motion this eve."

Before I could respond, the air shimmered once more. The temperature in the room plummeted, frost forming on the glasses behind the bar. The very foundations of Plazma seemed to tremble, and for a moment, I feared the structure wouldn't hold.

And then *he* was there.

Oberon Elegast stepped into Plazma as if he owned it. As if the very air should feel honored to touch his skin. His presence was overwhelming, a force of nature in physical form. He wore no crown and needed no ornate robes to declare his status. His power radiated from him in waves, causing the lights to flicker and the glasses behind the bar to vibrate ever so slightly.

But it was not Oberon who first caught my eye. It was the figure who entered just before him, announcing his arrival.

Beto.

My heart clenched painfully in my chest, a tangle of emotions so intense it left me breathless. He was breathtaking, dressed in a suit of deep forest green that seemed to shift and rustle like leaves in a breeze. His russet curls were crowned with a circlet of gold, delicate vines intertwining with the metal. But it was his eyes that captured me—those familiar green-gold orbs now blazed with an inner light, ancient and fathomless.

For a moment, just a moment, I saw uncertainty flicker in their depths as they met mine. Then his face smoothed into a mask of courtly detachment.

Time seemed to slow, the rest of the world fading away as I drank in the sight of him. How many nights had I lain awake, replaying our last encounter? How many times had I cursed his name, only to whisper it like a prayer in the dark hours before dawn?

Seeing him now, resplendent in his Fae glory, I felt a surge of conflicting emotions. Pride at the power he wielded, the respect he commanded. Anger at his betrayal, at the choices that had led us to this moment. Fear of what his presence here might mean. And beneath it all, a love so deep and true it terrified me.

I wanted to run to him, to feel his arms around me one last time. I wanted to scream at him, to demand answers for every hurt, every sleepless night. I wanted to beg him to choose me, to choose us, over his Fae obligations.

But I did none of these things. I was the Shard Keeper, and Vegas needed me to be strong. I could no more abandon my duties than he could his.

So I stood tall, met his gaze with all the dignity I could muster, and tried to ignore the way my heart raced at his proximity.

"My Lord Oberon Elegast, King-Consort of the Seelie Court, Ruler of the Green, Lord of the Wild Hunt," Beto announced, his voice ringing with power that sent shivers through the assembled crowd.

Oberon's eyes, black as the space between stars, found mine. A smile curved his lips, beautiful and terrifying. "Well met, little Shard Keeper," he purred, his voice like honey over broken glass. "Shall we begin? I do so hate to waste time on... pleasantries."

As I prepared to lead the Fae nobility to the negotiation space, Ambroginio stepped forward, every inch the gracious host despite the palpable tension in the air.

"Lord Oberon," he purred, offering a bow that was just a fraction too shallow to be entirely respectful.

"Welcome to Plazma. I trust you'll find our humble e stablishment... adequate for your needs."

Oberon's eyes narrowed, a dangerous glint in their fathomless depths. "Ambroginio," he acknowledged coldly. "Still playing at being a power in this realm, I see. How... quaint."

I felt the temperature in the room drop several degrees and saw Ambroginio's fingers twitch as if longing to form claws.

"Now, now, Your Grace," Ambroginio replied, his voice honey-sweet but with a razor's edge beneath. "Let's not forget the rules of hospitality. You are a guest in my domain, after all."

Oberon's laugh was like ice cracking. "Your domain? A paltry nightclub in a city barely older than a blink of my eye? You overstep, blood-drinker."

"And you forget yourself, Faerie King," Ambroginio shot back, all pretense of civility gone. "This 'paltry nightclub' stands as neutral ground, sanctioned by powers older than even you. Or have you forgotten the accords that bind us all?"

Oberon's gaze swept the room, his lip curling in disdain. "This...will serve. Though I had thought the Shard Keeper's offices were the traditional venue for such meetings. Or have you misplaced them, little one?"

I felt a surge of anger at his condescending tone, but I kept my voice level as I replied, "The destruction of my offices, as I'm sure you're well aware, Your Grace, necessitated alternative arrangements."

Oberon's smile was all teeth. "Ah yes, that unfortunate incident. How... clumsy of you."

I took a step forward, drawing on every ounce of authority I possessed. "Let me be clear, Lord Oberon. As Shard Keeper, I have the power to declare any area within the city limits as neutral ground for official business. I have done so with Plazma for the duration of these negotiations."

The air crackled with tension as Oberon and I locked eyes. For a moment, I thought he might challenge me outright. Then, to my surprise, he threw back his head and laughed.

"Well, well," he chuckled, though there was no warmth in the sound. "It seems our little Shard Keeper has grown a spine. Very well, child. Let us see if your authority holds as much weight as you believe it does."

As we moved towards the negotiation table, I caught Ambroginio's approving nod. It was a minor victory, but in this dangerous game, I'd take what I could get.

I led the Fae nobility to the prepared negotiation space, a circular table carved from a single piece of ancient oak.

Where the hell did Ambroginio find this?

As they took their seats, I couldn't help but marvel at the distinction between Tatiyana and Oberon. She was winter's first frost, beautiful but deadly. He was the wild heart of the forest, unpredictable and primal.

As the Fae settled, I caught a flicker of movement from the corner of my eye. Nicky had stepped forward, ostensibly to adjust one item hanging on the wall, but her gaze was locked on Tatiyana.

For a heartbeat, the world stopped.

Tatiyana's eyes met Nicky's, and the mask of cold nobility slipped. In its place was a look of such raw longing that it took my breath away. Nicky's hand trembled, reaching out almost involuntarily before she caught herself.

The air between them crackled with unspoken words, with memories of a stolen moment that should never have been. I saw Tatiyana's fingers twitch, as if fighting the urge to reach across the divide of mortality and magic that separated them.

Nicky's lips parted, a whisper of "My Lady" barely audible in the tense silence.

Tatiyana's response was equally soft, a breathed "Nicolette" that carried the weight of centuries of regret.

The moment stretched, fragile as spun glass and just as dangerous. I saw confusion on the faces of the other Fae, saw the dawning realization in Beto's eyes.

And then Oberon's voice shattered the spell.

"Come now, wife," he sneered, the word dripping with disdain. "Surely you're not still pining after your little mortal pet?"

Tatiyana's face snapped back to its regal mask, but not before I saw a flash of pain in her eyes. Nicky stumbled back as if struck, her face flushing with a mixture of shame and anger.

"You will hold your tongue, Oberon," Tatiyana hissed, frost forming on her fingertips. "Or I shall remove it."

Oberon's laugh was cruel. "Oh? And add that to your collection of mortal trinkets? How unsurprising."

I stepped forward, desperate to regain control of the situation. "Your Graces, please. We're here to negotiate, not to dredge up old wounds."

But the damage was done. The tenuous balance we'd struck had been upended, and I could feel the negotiations sliding further out of reach.

Nicky retreated to the far side of the room. But I could see the tremble in her hands, the way her eyes kept darting to Tatiyana despite her best efforts.

My stomach knotted at the pain I was putting her through.

Tatiyana, for her part, had drawn her power around her like armor. But beneath the icy exterior, I sensed a deep, aching vulnerability. A reminder that even beings as ancient and powerful as the Fae were not immune to the complexities of the heart.

"Before we begin," I began, my voice steadier than I felt, "I would remind all parties that this is neutral ground. Tradition will enforce that neutrality."

Oberon's laugh was like the wind through autumn leaves. "Such precautions, little one. Do you fear us so?"

"Respect is not fear, Your Grace," I countered, "And wisdom often lies in preparation."

Tatiyana's lips curved in a small smile. "Well said, Shard Keeper. Now, to the matter at hand. The child."

"The child is mine by right of tithe," Oberon stated, all pretense of amusement gone from his voice. "A tithe offered, and a bargain struck."

"A bargain made under duress is no bargain at all," Tatiyana shot back, frost forming on the rim of her water glass. "The mother was imprisoned, vulnerable. You took advantage."

I could feel the temperature in the room dropping and saw the shadows lengthening as Oberon's anger grew. This was spiraling out of control faster than I'd expected.

"Your Graces," I interjected, "perhaps we might consider the intent behind the tithe, rather than the letter of the agreement?"

Both Fae turned to look at me, their gazes intense enough to make me want to shrink back. But I held my ground.

"The purpose of a changeling tithe is to bring fresh blood, new power into your courts," I continued, silently thanking both Malik for his insights. "Power that the City did not grant to your Kin, I would remind you both. Your Court was not gifted the blessing of increase. But perhaps there is another way to honor the gifted tithe."

Oberon's eyes narrowed. "Explain."

I took a deep breath. "What if, instead of claiming the child, you were to become mentors ... godparents of a sort? There are plenty of stories where various Kin have served in this role as an example."

"You wish me to become a Fairy Godfather ... Absurd," Oberon scoffed, but I saw a flicker of interest in Tatiyana's eyes.

"It... has... been done before, yes," Tatiyana mused. "We did so for several hundred years in France, if you recall."

"It would dilute our power," Oberon growled.

"Or it could broaden your influence as the child grows," I pressed. "Bringing in new perspectives, new adaptations. The world is changing, Your Grace. Perhaps the Fae must change with it."

Oberon leaned forward, his eyes boring into mine. "And what do you know of change, little Shard Keeper? You, who are but a beat in the heart of eternity? I have seen empires rise and fall, watched as your kind crawled from the muck and dared to dream. And through it all, we have endured. We have thrived."

"At what cost?" I challenged, emboldened by desperation. "How many children have you taken, Your Grace? How many families have you torn apart in the name of tradition?"

The silence that followed was deafening. I saw shock on the faces of the Fae retinue and something like grudging respect in Tatiyana's eyes. And Beto... Beto looked at me with a mixture of pride and fear that made my heart ache.

Oberon stood slowly, his chair scraping back with a sound like tearing flesh. "You dare," he said softly, dangerously. "You dare to question our ways, our very nature?"

"I dare to enforce the limitations of increase as is my right as Shard Keeper. I dare to hope for a better future," I replied, standing my ground even as every instinct screamed at me to run.

For a moment, I thought I'd gotten through to him. But then Oberon's power surged, a tidal wave of ancient magic that threatened to overwhelm us all.

"Enough of this foolishness," he snarled. "The child is mine by right. I will not be denied."

The air crackled with power, and I saw Tatiyana rising to meet the challenge, her own magic swirling around her like a storm.

"Your Grace, please," I started, but my words were drowned out by the rising wind that howled through the club.

Glasses shattered. The lights flickered and died. And in the darkness, I heard Oberon's voice, cold and cruel.

"You've made a grave mistake, little Shard Keeper. Now, you'll learn the price of defying the Fae."

As chaos erupted around me, I felt a moment of utter despair. I'd failed. The City, the child, everything was about to pay the price for my arrogance.

But then, through the maelstrom, I felt a warm hand grasp mine. I turned to see Beto, his eyes glowing with an inner fire.

"It's not over," he whispered. "Trust me."

"Beto," I gasped, "what are you doing?"

His eyes met mine, filled with a determination I'd never seen before. "What I should have done from the beginning. Protecting the Shard. Protecting you."

With a gesture, Beto crafted a protective barrier, encompassing Nicky, Tom, Quincey, and Cozy. The DaVinci crew huddled together, their faces a mixture of awe and terror as they watched the supernatural storm rage around us.

"Father!" Beto's voice cut through the chaos, ringing with an authority that made even Oberon pause. "This ends now."

Oberon's face contorted with rage. "You dare defy me, boy? Have you forgotten who gave you power, who made you what you are?"

"I haven't forgotten," Beto replied, his voice steady. "But I remember something else, too. Something you taught me long ago, though I doubt you meant for me to apply it like this."

Confusion flickered across Oberon's face. "What nonsense is this?"

Beto stepped forward, placing himself between Oberon and me. "The law of intent, Father. The foundation of all Fae contracts and magic. You've always said that intent fashions the letter of any agreement."

I saw understanding dawn in Tatiyana's eyes. But before she could speak, Oberon's patience snapped.

"Enough!" he roared, his power surging once more. "I will not be lectured by my son, nor will I allow this farce to continue. The child is mine, as is my right. And if you stand in my way, Shard Keeper, I will tear this city apart stone by stone until I have what is mine."

The negotiations had well and truly collapsed. As Oberon's magic lashed out, threatening to overwhelm even Beto's protective barrier, I braced myself for the worst.

Humans Ammirit?

There are moments in your life when you are in the thick of things and a tiny voice says, "So this is how I die..."

That was the voice I was hearing in my head at that moment.

The air in Plazma crackled with enough raw power to choke on. Oberon's fury manifested as a tempest of ancient magic, his will pressing against the very foundations of Ambroginio's club. Each pulse of power made the lights flare and sputter like dying neon.

He'd already destroyed one sanctuary this week. The Kinship's laws were clear about violating neutral ground - but he seemed beyond caring about consequences now.

Through Plazma's windows, I caught glimpses of mounted figures circling the building. Their horses' hooves never quite touched the ground, their riders' forms flickering between human and something far more ancient and terrible. The Wild Hunt - Oberon's personal army - awaiting their master's command.

Jesus, I hated this fucker.

Beto's protective magic shimmered around us, a gossamer-thin shield of light that seemed impossibly fragile against his father's onslaught. I could see the strain on his face, sweat beading on his brow as he fought to maintain the protection.

Tatiyana stood resolute, her own power a swirling vortex of winter's fury, but even she seemed dwarfed by Oberon's unleashed might. The fate of a child, of our city, of the delicate balance between mortal and Fae realms - it all hung by a thread, and that thread was unraveling before our eyes.

"Your Grace," Ambroginio's voice cut through the chaos, all pretense of theatricality gone. "You stand in violation of sacred law. This ground is neutral by declaration of the Shard Keeper and the agreement of the Kinship. Your actions here will have... consequences."

The temperature dropped further as Oberon's laughter echoed through the club. "Consequences? You dare threaten me with your petty laws? I am Oberon Elegast, Lord of the Wild Hunt! Your rules mean nothing to me!"

"Then you declare yourself outlaw," Tatiyana's voice rang with formal power. "You stand apart from Court and Kin. Is this truly your choice, husband?"

I frantically searched for a solution, my mind racing through possibilities, each more desperate than the last. But I came up empty. We were out of options, out of time.

And then, cutting through the maelstrom like a beacon in the darkest night, a single word:

"Stop!"

The voice rang out, clear and strong, silencing even the howling magical winds. I turned, disbelieving, to see Nicky stepping forward. Her face was set in grim determination, chin lifted in defiance of the supernatural chaos surrounding us. The scars on her wrists - remnants of that terrible night years ago - seemed to catch the flickering light of the dying neon.

"Nicky, don't!" I cried, horror gripping my heart as she moved beyond the safety of Beto's protection. I saw Tom reach for his sister, panic etched on his face, but Quincey held him back, understanding dawning in his eyes.

Oberon's magic swirled around her, tendrils of power caressing her skin with deadly promise. But Nicky stood tall, unflinching in the face of a being who could unmake her with a thought. Her eyes, once filled with fear at the mere mention of the Fae, now blazed with a determination I'd never seen before.

"Lord Oberon Elegast," she said, her voice steady despite the chaos, carrying an authority I'd never heard from her before. "I call in my favor."

The words hung in the air, heavy with meaning and ancient power. Suddenly, impossibly, the magical storm ceased. It was as if someone had hit a cosmic pause button, leaving us in a bubble of unnatural stillness.

Oberon's eyes widened in shock, then narrowed dangerously. The temperature in the room plummeted, frost creeping across the floors and walls.

"What did you say, mortal?" he hissed, his voice dripping with equal parts disbelief and venom.

Nicky met his gaze unflinchingly. "You heard me. Years ago, in a hospital room that reeked of antiseptic and broken dreams, you made me an offer. Do you remember, Your Grace? You said you'd make the pain go away, make me forget. But there was a price."

I saw Tatiyana flinch at these words, a flicker of guilt crossing her face. Beto looked stricken, no doubt remembering his own role in those events.

Nicky continued, her voice growing stronger with each word. "I didn't take your offer then. I chose to remember, to carry the weight of what happened. And in doing so, I bound you to a debt. Because what happened to me... was your fault. A debt I'm calling in now."

The air crackled with tension as the full implications of Nicky's words sank in. This wasn't just about one favor - it was about years of trauma, of lives forever altered by Fae machinations. It was about a mortal standing up to a god-like being, armed with nothing but the strength of her conviction and the power of a promise made in a moment of vulnerability.

Oberon's face contorted with rage, but I could see the trapped look in his eyes. He was bound by his own laws, caught in a web of his own making.

"What would you ask of me, mortal?" he spat, each word dripping with venom.

"I ask that you relinquish all claim to the child." Nicky's voice rang out, clear and strong. "That you grant full custody to Lady Tatiyana, with no strings attached, no loopholes, no tricks."

A ripple moved through the assembled Kin. I felt it too - the weight of what we were witnessing. This wasn't just Nicky standing up to Oberon. This was humanity itself, refusing to be pawns any longer in the games of the Kin.

For centuries, perhaps millennia, the supernatural had used humans as playthings, as resources to be exploited. They had manipulated our dreams, fed on our fears, and twisted our lives to suit their whims. But here, now, in a nightclub in the heart of Las Vegas, that age-old dynamic was being challenged.

"You dare?" Oberon's voice was soft, dangerous. "You would use Fae law against me? Have you forgotten who I am, what I am capable of?"

"No," Nicky replied, standing her ground. "I remember exactly who you are. What you are. And that's why I know you can't refuse."

The room fell silent, all eyes on Oberon. The ancient Fae lord stood frozen, centuries of power and authority crashing against the immovable object of his own laws. I could see the fury building in him, like a storm gathering strength.

"So be it," he growled, the words torn from him against his will. "The child is yours, Tatiyana. May you choke on your victory."

With those words, I felt a shift in the air, as if an unseen contract had been sealed. Reality seemed to shudder, acknowledging the pact. Tatiyana's face lit up with fierce joy, while Oberon darkened with a fury that promised disaster for any who crossed his path.

His gaze swept the room, promising retribution, before settling on his son. The temperature dropped even further as he took a menacing step toward Robert.

"And you, my son," Oberon's voice was soft, but laced with centuries of barely contained rage. "My heir. My greatest creation. How does it feel to betray your own blood?"

Robert stood tall, his jaw set and eyes blazing with a mixture of defiance and sorrow. "I didn't betray our blood, Father. I honored it."

Oberon's laugh was cruel, devoid of any warmth. "Honor? Oh, my foolish boy. Everything you are, everything you have - it's because of me. I molded you from nothing, gave you power beyond mortal comprehension. And this is how you repay me? By siding with these... insects?"

The air crackled with tension as father and son faced each other. I could see the conflict in Robert's eyes, centuries of loyalty warring with his newfound convictions.

"You're wrong, Father," Robert said, his voice steady despite the emotion I could see roiling beneath the surface. "These 'insects' have shown me more about honor, about true strength, than all your centuries of manipulation ever did."

Oberon's face contorted with fury. The lights of Plazma flickered and died, leaving only the glow of neon from the street outside to illuminate the scene. His form seemed to grow larger, more primal - not through magic, but through the sheer force of his rage.

"You are no son of mine," he snarled. "You are weak, corrupted by mortal sentiment. When the time comes, remember that you chose this path. Remember that you turned your back on your heritage, on your destiny."

Ambroginio stepped forward then, his usual theatrical manner replaced by something ancient and deadly. "Lord Oberon, you have violated neutral ground twice now. You have rejected your heir before witnesses. By the laws that bind all Kin, there must be a reckoning."

"A reckoning?" Oberon's laugh was sharp as broken glass. "You dare speak to me of reckonings, blood-drinker? Very well. Let there be a reckoning. But remember - you chose this. All of you."

His gaze swept the room once more, lingering on each face in turn: Tatiyana, standing proud and victorious. Nicky, still refusing to back down. The DaVinci crew, united in their defiance. Me, the Shard Keeper he had failed to intimidate. And finally, Robert, the son he was casting aside.

"You are dead to me, boy," he said, his voice dropping to a whisper that somehow carried more menace than any shout. "Pray we never meet again."

With that, Oberon turned and strode toward the door. No magical portal, no dramatic disappearance - just the King of the Wild Hunt walking out into the Las Vegas night. But somehow, that was more terrifying than any supernatural display could have been.

The tension in the room held for several heartbeats after he left. Then, slowly, it began to dissipate, leaving us all breathing easier but far from relaxed.

"The Courts will need to be notified," Tatiyana said, breaking the silence. "His actions here... there will be consequences."

"He knows," Ambroginio replied grimly. "Why do you think he walked out that door instead of vanishing? He's declaring his independence from our laws. From all of us."

"Then he is truly outlaw," Tatiyana's voice carried the weight of a formal declaration. "Let it be known among all Kin of Vegas - Oberon Elegast stands apart from Court and Law. He is denied sanctuary and succor within our territories."

I looked at Robert, seeing the pain those words caused him. Whatever else Oberon was, he was still Robert's father. Centuries of history, of loyalty, of family - all severed in a single night.

"Beto," I started, but he held up a hand, stopping me.

"Don't," he said softly. "Just... don't."

The silence following Tatiyana's formal declaration was broken by movement. Nicky swayed slightly, the adrenaline clearly fading and leaving exhaustion in its wake. I moved to support her, but Tatiyana was faster.

"Nicolette," she breathed, reaching Nicky in two swift strides. The formal mask of the Fae Queen cracked, revealing raw emotion beneath. Her hands trembled as she reached for Nicky's face, cupping it gently between her palms. Their eyes met and held, and the air between them crackled with unspoken words and long-buried feelings.

"My brave, foolish mortal," Tatiyana whispered, her thumb gently stroking Nicky's cheek. "After everything... after all this time... you still found the strength to stand."

"How could I not?" Nicky whispered back, her voice thick with emotion. "I couldn't let him take another child. Couldn't let him break another family."

A single tear traced down Tatiyana's perfect porcelain cheek. She leaned forward, pressing her forehead against Nicky's. "You have my protection," she said, her voice carrying the weight of formal declaration even as it trembled with personal meaning. "Against him. Against any who would harm you."

She pulled back slightly, pressing her lips to Nicky's forehead in a gesture of blessing. Then she turned to face the DaVinci crew, though she kept one hand firmly clasped with Nicky's.

"You all have my protection," the Laird of Las Vegas declared. "Each of you. I know what you risked tonight - the enmity of my Consort is no small thing. But know that from this moment forward, you stand under the aegis of my Court. Until such time as I draw my last breath, you and yours will have sanctuary among us."

The weight of her words settled over the room like a mantle. This wasn't just political maneuvering or the repayment of a debt. This was something deeper, more personal - a promise born of regret, of recognition, of respect.

The moment was shattered by the crash of Ambroginio's doors flying open.

"My Lord! The Library - it's under attack!"

The messenger's words hung in the air for a heartbeat. Then everything moved at once.

"Of course," Ambroginio growled, all pretense of civility vanishing. "He's not just declaring himself outlaw - he's trying to erase the very laws that bind him."

"We will secure Plazma and rally the Courts," Tatiyana said to me. "Someone must make the formal declarations to both Seelie and Unseelie Courts, and the rest of the Kin - as Laird, that duty falls to me. The balance of power is shifting, and we cannot afford any question of legitimacy in what comes next."

I looked to Robert, who stood staring at the door his father had walked through moments ago. The weight of centuries seemed to press down on his shoulders.

"Beto," I said softly. "We need to move."

He turned to me, and in his eyes, I saw something change. The last traces of the dutiful son fell away, replaced by determination tinged with anger. "The Library," he said. "That's where he'll be. Not his forces - him personally. He'll want to destroy the records himself."

"Then that's where we'll face him," I replied, trying to project more confidence than I felt.

"Shard Keeper," Ambroginio called as we headed for the door. "Remember our bargain. The price for my hospitality may soon come due."

I nodded grimly. One problem at a time. First, we had to stop Oberon from destroying centuries of knowledge and contracts. Then we could worry about my growing debt to a Blood-Kin.

Behind us, I heard Tatiyana speaking rapidly, issuing commands to her people. The DaVinci crew huddled together, Nicky still holding the Laird's hand as if it were a lifeline. They had fought their battle, and stood their ground. Now it was our turn.

"Ready?" I asked Beto as we stepped out into the neon-lit night.

His smile was sharp as broken glass. "Time to show my father what his 'weak' son can really do."

We ran into the darkness, leaving behind one battlefield for another. Above us, the Vegas sky blazed with artificial stars, oblivious to the war about to erupt in its shadows.

The night wasn't over yet. Not by a long shot.

Go Time

The Wild Hunt was tearing up Las Vegas Boulevard, and all I could think was: the insurance paperwork on this is going to be hell.

Ancient hunters on supernatural steeds thundered between the neon and glass canyons of the Strip, while tourists stumbled out of their way, phones raised to capture what they probably thought was some new Cirque show. The riders shifted between shadow and light, their forms fluid as casino revenue, their horses' hooves striking sparks from concrete that shimmered like slots paying out.

Welcome to Vegas, where even the apocalypse comes with a floor show.

"Faster," Beto urged as we ran. His voice carried an edge I'd never heard before - something between fury and fear. "If he gets into the deep archives..."

"He won't," I said, though my lungs were burning. Turns out being a Shard Keeper doesn't automatically make you Olympic athlete material. Who knew? "Amrita will have locked down-"

A horn blast cut through the night - deep, primal, and carrying harmonics that would have made a Cirque sound designer weep with envy. The Hunt was calling its master.

"They've found a way in," Beto said grimly.

We rounded the corner to the Library's facade, and I felt my heart drop. The historic storefront was intact, its "Museum" sign still proclaiming "Open By Appointment Only" in faded letters. But shadows writhed around its edges like a bad night at the sports book, and three riders held positions outside, their mounts pawing at the air as if it were solid ground. Above the entrance, frost patterns crawled across the brick.

"Dad's already inside," Beto said, pulling me into the shelter of a doorway. "Those are just our welcoming committee."

"Please tell me you've got a plan that doesn't involve us charging the immortal hunting party."

His smile was sharp in the darkness. "They're bound to him by choice and ancient magic. I'm bound by blood. Let's see which is stronger."

Before I could point out all the ways this could go wrong, Beto stepped out of the shadows and called out: "Brothers of the Hunt! Will you deny passage to your lord's son?"

Movement caught my eye - a group of figures emerging from a side street. Andy Mak led the charge, his massive frame somehow more imposing in an LVFD uniform than when he was half-shifted to wolf form. Behind him came a mix of firefighters and police, some human, some very much not.

"Any chance of keeping this contained?" he called over to us, eyeing the riders with clear distaste.

"Working on it," I replied. One of the Hunt's horses snorted, breathing out clouds that looked suspiciously like winter storm warnings.

"Goddamn Fae and their goddamn drama," Andy muttered, then turned to his people. "Alright, listen up! I want a perimeter three blocks out. Work with Metro - gas leak story. Martin, get your people on crowd control. Last thing we need is this showing up on TikTok."

A sleek black woman in Metro blues - definitely one of the big cat Shifters by her movement - grinned. "Already trending, boss. #VegasWildHunt."

"Wonderful." Andy's voice dripped sarcasm. "Because that's exactly what we need. Social media influencers chasing down the Wild Hunt for likes."

One of the mounted Fae warriors turned toward us, his armor shifting like oil on water. "This doesn't concern you, beast-blood. Stand aside."

I saw Andy's shoulders tense, but his voice stayed professional. "Actually, friend, it does concern me. See this?" He tapped his LVFD badge. "Means I protect this city. ALL of this city. So unless you've got a permit for this little parade..."

Behind him, I saw his people spreading out with practiced efficiency. Uniforms or not, these were predators moving to contain a threat. The Hunt's horses stamped restlessly, picking up on the tension.

"The old laws-" the Fae warrior began, but Andy cut him off.

"Mean jack shit when there's civilians in the crossfire. Now, you want to chase each other around the desert? Fine. But this is my city too, and I've got a job to do."

I felt a surge of pride at his words. This was what I'd hoped for - the Kin stepping up not just for territory or power, but for Vegas itself.

"He's right," Beto called out, his voice carrying the weight of command. "The Hunt was never meant for mortal cities. You know this, brothers."

The mounted warriors exchanged looks. I could practically see the balance of power shifting, ancient protocols warring with modern necessity.

A burst of radio static broke the tension. "Sir, we've got rubberneckers trying to get past the barricade on Fremont. Claiming they're with 'Paranormal Vegas Tours.'"

Andy pinched the bridge of his nose. "Of course we do. Send them to the Mob Museum instead." He looked back at the Hunt. "Well? What's it gonna be? Because I've got actual fires to deal with after this, and my overtime's already maxed out."

The mounted Fae warrior drew himself up, clearly preparing for some grand pronouncement about ancient rights and eternal hunts. I'd been dealing with supernatural politics long enough to recognize the signs of an incoming monologue.

Nope. Not tonight.

"Enough." I stepped forward, feeling Vegas pulse through me like a bass line at three AM. "Oberon Elegast stands outlaw from Court and Kin. The Laird herself has declared it." The neon-tinged night seemed to deepen around us as I spoke. "That means his Hunt has no rights here. No authority here."

I felt it then - that connection Dean had tried to explain to me all those months ago. The city wasn't just buildings and streets. It was every desperate gambler's dream, every showgirl's ambition, every working stiff's determination to make it through one more shift. It was three AM pancakes and midnight marriages, jackpot bells and last call warnings.

It was mine to protect.

"This is my city," I said, my voice carrying the weight of every slot machine's ding and every dealer's call. "Your master violated neutral ground, attacked the Library, and threatened my people. So let me make this very clear."

I took another step forward. The Hunt's horses shifted nervously.

"Get. Off. My. City. Skin."

Power rippled through the street - not magic, but something older. Something that belonged to Vegas itself. The neon seemed to pulse in time with my heartbeat, and for just a moment, I swore I could feel every light on the Strip.

The lead rider's mount reared, its hooves striking sparks from nothing. But these weren't the showy sparks from before. These looked almost... afraid.

"The Shard has spoken," Beto said into the silence that followed. His voice carried both pride and warning. "I suggest you choose your next move carefully, brothers."

Andy's people had moved into position during my little speech. Shifters trying to look casual while coiled for action, their badges catching the street light. Vegas's protectors, supernatural and mundane, united.

The Hunt's leader looked from me to Andy to his fellow riders, clearly doing the math. Finally, he inclined his head - not quite a bow, but close enough.

"We hear and acknowledge the Shard's decree," he said formally. Then, less formally: "But your problem's still inside, Keeper. And he's not going to listen nearly so well."

I managed not to roll my eyes. Barely. "Yeah, well, that's a family matter. Right, Beto?"

Beto's smile was sharp as a poker player's tell. "Indeed. Shall we go talk to my father about proper library etiquette?"

The hidden door behind the fake museum display swung open silently. I half-expected to find the stairway frozen over, given Oberon's flair for dramatics. Instead, the air was warm - unnaturally so. Like a desert wind had somehow found its way underground.

"He's burning the archives," Beto said grimly. His face was tight with anger, but I caught something else in his expression - fear? "We need to hurry."

Andy had his people securing the perimeter, making sure Oberon's theatrics didn't end up on the evening news. Just another night in Vegas - nothing to see here folks, move along, ignore the fairy king throwing a tantrum in the basement.

We descended the stairs, our footsteps echoing despite our attempts at stealth. The familiar smell of old books and older magic grew stronger with each step, but now it was tainted with something acrid.

"Amrita?" I called out softly.

"Here." Her voice came from the shadows. She emerged looking decidedly un-Amrita-like - her usual pristine appearance was disheveled, her white suit stained with what looked like ash. "I've managed to secure the most critical texts, but he's determined. And he knows exactly what he's looking for."

"The contracts," Beto said. It wasn't a question.

"Yes. Specifically, the original bindings between the Fae Courts and the City." Amrita's eyes met mine. "The ones that limit their power here. The ones that give the Shard authority over them."

Well, shit.

A crash echoed from deeper in the Library, followed by the distinctive sound of shelves toppling. Amrita flinched as if she'd been struck.

"Dad always did hate research," Beto muttered. Then, to me: "Ready?"

I thought about Dean and his lessons on being a Shard Keeper. About balance and duty and knowing when to fight. About the City that had chosen me, that pulsed through my veins like neon and starlight.

"One thing first," I said, and kissed him.

It wasn't a goodbye kiss. It wasn't even really a good luck kiss. It was a promise - to him, to myself, to Vegas. Whatever happened next, whatever price we had to pay, we'd face it together.

When we broke apart, his eyes were glowing faintly in the darkness. "Well then," he said softly. "Shall we go disappoint my father one last time?"

"After you, Your Highness."

We stepped into the heart of the Library, ready to face whatever came next. Above us, the Vegas sky blazed on, oblivious to the war in its shadows.

Some nights you hit the jackpot. Some nights you go bust.

And some nights you have to stop a fairy king from burning down the supernatural card catalog.

The deeper sections of the Library looked like someone had tried to recreate Dante's Inferno using rare books as kindling. Shelves lay toppled like fallen dominoes, their contents scattered across the floor. The air was thick with ash and the peculiar smell of burning contracts - like ozone mixed with broken promises.

And there, in the center of it all, stood Oberon Elegast. His form seemed larger somehow in the confined space, antlers scraping the ceiling, shadows writhing around him like living things. In his hands, he held what looked like an ancient ledger bound in something I really didn't want to identify.

"I was wondering when you'd arrive," he said, not looking up from the book. "Come to watch me free us all from these tedious restrictions?"

"Actually," I replied, "I'm here to file a complaint about your late fees."

Now he did look up, and his smile was terrible to behold. "Ah, the Shard Keeper attempts humor. How charming. And my son..." His gaze shifted to Beto, and the temperature in the room plummeted. "Come to die with your pet humans?"

"No, Father." Beto's voice was steady, though I saw his hands clench at his sides. "I've come to stop you from making a terrible mistake."

Oberon laughed, and the sound made my teeth ache. "Mistake? I'm correcting a mistake, boy. These bindings, these limitations - they're chains, nothing more. We are creatures of magic and dream! We should not be bound by mortal laws and petty agreements!"

"Those agreements keep the peace," Amrita said from somewhere behind us. "They protect both sides-"

"They make us weak!" Oberon roared. The ledger in his hands began to smoke. "Look at what we've become! Playing nice with mongrels and blood-drinkers, pretending at civilization when we should rule it all!"

"Yeah, about that," I cut in because apparently I'd left my self-preservation instincts upstairs. "How's that working out for you? Last I checked, you're the one who's the outlaw. Seems like the system's working just fine."

His eyes fixed on me, ancient and cold as space between stars. "You think your proclamations mean anything? Your petty authority?" He raised the ledger. "Once I destroy the original contracts, all of it becomes meaningless. The Shard's power, the territorial agreements, everything. Vegas will be mine to rule as I see fit."

"You really don't get it, do you?" I took a step forward, feeling Vegas pulse through me like a winning hand. "This City doesn't belong to you. It doesn't even belong to me. It belongs to everyone who's ever dropped their last dollar in a slot machine hoping for a miracle. Everyone who's ever come here looking for a second chance. Everyone who calls this neon oasis home."

"Pretty words," Oberon sneered. "But words won't stop me from-"

"No," Beto interrupted. "But I will."

Power crackled between father and son, but not the showy magical display I'd come to expect from the Fae. This was older, deeper - the weight of blood and birthright and bitter truths.

"You think you can stop me?" Oberon's voice held something I hadn't heard before - uncertainty. "You're nothing without the power I gave you. Nothing without my blood."

"Your blood." Beto's laugh was harsh. "That's all it's ever been about, hasn't it? Blood and power and control." He stepped forward, and for the first time, I saw Oberon take a step back. "But you forgot something, Father. Something important."

"Oh?" Oberon's grip on the ledger tightened. "And what's that?"

"I'm your son. Your blood. Which means I know exactly how you think." Beto's hands moved in a complex gesture. "And I know exactly where you bound your own contract."

Oberon's eyes widened. "You wouldn't dare-"

"Watch me." Beto's words carried the weight of centuries. "By blood and bone, by birth and binding, I call you to account, Father."

The air itself seemed to tear open behind Oberon - not with magic or power, but with the inexorable pull of Faerie responding to one of its own. The ledger dropped from his hands as he staggered.

"What have you done?" he snarled.

"Called in a debt older than Vegas." Beto's voice was grim. "The price of creating me. You have to answer for it - in Faerie itself."

The portal widened, hungry darkness reaching for Oberon. He fought against it, but I could see the battle was already lost.

"Beto," I started, realizing what this meant. "Don't-"

"I have to." He turned to me, and in his eyes, I saw centuries of love and regret. "He'll keep coming back unless someone makes him answer for everything. For all of it." His smile was sad. "Guess it's time for a long-overdue family reunion."

"But-"

"I'll find my way back to you," he promised. "However long it takes."

Then he stepped forward and shoved his father, hard. They both tumbled into the darkness, Oberon's roar of rage cut off as the portal snapped shut behind them.

The silence that followed was deafening.

The ledger lay forgotten on the floor, slightly singed but intact. Around us, the Library seemed to exhale, the unnatural heat dissipating.

"Well," Amrita said softly. "That's going to complicate things."

I picked up the ledger, trying to ignore the way my hands shook. "Will he..." I couldn't finish the question.

"Find his way back?" Amrita's voice was gentle. "Eventually. But time moves differently in Faerie, especially when there are debts to be settled. And this..." She gestured at the devastation around us. "This was a very large debt indeed."

Above us, Vegas pulsed on, unaware that its newest protector had sacrificed everything to keep it safe. To keep me safe.

Some nights, the house always wins.

But sometimes, the real cost of winning is higher than anyone expected.

Clean-up took hours—not just the physical mess—though there was plenty of that—but the political fallout. Amrita and I cataloged every damaged text and every scorched contract while Andy's people managed the chaos upstairs. Apparently, "gas leak" only goes so far as an explanation when half the Strip has spotted mythological creatures doing stunt riding between the casinos.

"Instagram's going to be a nightmare," Amrita muttered, carefully restoring a singed ledger to its shelf. "Though I suppose that's better than TikTok. Last thing we need is the Wild Hunt becoming a dance challenge."

I managed a weak laugh, though my heart wasn't in it. Every few minutes, my eyes drifted to the spot where the portal had been. Where Beto had been.

"He'll come back," Amrita said softly, catching my look. "Though I suspect Oberon will not. At least, not as we knew him."

"The Kinship?"

"Will adapt. They always do." She straightened her ash-stained suit. "He destroyed two neutral meeting places and attacked a sacred Library. Not as dire as allowing an entire City to fall, but he will have a rough landing wherever he goes. Tatiyana's position is stronger now. Between this and her protection of the DaVinci crew... well, let's just say the balance of power has shifted significantly."

I nodded, too tired to fully process the implications. One crisis at a time.

By the time we emerged from the Library, dawn was breaking. The Vegas sky was turning from black to purple to pink, the neon finally giving way to natural light. Andy waited outside with coffee—the good stuff, not vending machine sludge.

"Thought you might need this," he said, handing me a cup. "Hell of a night."

"Hell of a night," I agreed. "Thank you. For everything."

He shrugged. "It's what we do. Protect the city." His eyes met mine. "All of us."

I felt Vegas pulse through me - tired but unbroken. Changed, maybe, but still standing. Still spinning its tales of luck and chance and second chances.

"Shard Keeper." Amrita's voice pulled me from my thoughts. "There is one other matter we should discuss. Your debt to Ambroginio..."

I held up a hand. "Tomorrow. Or today. Whatever this is. Right now, I need sleep, a shower, and maybe a drink. Not necessarily in that order."

She nodded, a small smile playing at her lips. "Very well. Though you should know - things are changing. The old alliances, the old rules... what happened here tonight will have consequences."

"It already has," I said softly, thinking of Beto.

Above us, the sun continued its rise over the City of Second Chances. In the distance, slot machines chimed their eternal song of hope and probability. It's a new day in Vegas, where everyone's looking for their own magic.

I just hadn't expected finding mine would mean losing it quite so soon.

But that's Vegas for you. The house doesn't always win - but the game never really ends.

You just have to know when to hold, when to fold, and when to bet everything on a promise whispered in the dark.

Beto would find his way back. And until then, I had a city to protect.

After all, it was mine now. Every light, every dream, every desperate prayer to Lady Luck.

All of it.

For better or worse, 'til death do us part.

Welcome to Vegas, baby. The show must go on.

About the author

SandDancer Publications

C.S. Kading and Tony Fuentes have been working together and crafting stories for over two decades. Partners in both mischief and memories, this dynamic duo combines real-world experience with formal education, to bring you stories to tickle your imagination and delight your hearts.

SandDancer was born out of the pandemic and a need to stay sane. We could not enjoy the company of others beyond the safety of our bubble, so we came to you the only other way we could - through books and storytelling.

The Authors

C.S. Kading

Literary Titan Gold Award-Winning Author

Charmain is a poet, playwright, and storyteller, whose love for writing began in 3rd grade when she won a district writing contest. Her love for fantastical forces motivates her to create stories of heroes, villains, gods, and monsters that often have a foundation in Old World mythology and legends.

MAED

Member: IASFA, IAN

indie B.R.A.G. Medallion recipient

Tony Fuentes

Literary Titan Gold Award-Winning Author

Tony is Renaissance Man in Geek's clothing; not only an author with a weird imagination, but also a painter, gamer, and part-time occultist. With his writing, he tries to spin humor into the world's grounded reality. At the same, he tries to get the audience to look into the stars and dream further beyond. In all things, he strives to give the weird and the wondrous things a place in the world for all to enjoy.

B.S. COMM

Member: IASFA

indie B.R.A.G. Medallion recipient

Also by

<u>SandDancer Publications</u>

https://sanddancer.pub/

<u>Sin City Shard Chronicles</u>

House of Cards

<u>The Realm of Gothika</u>

Raise the Dead (a love story)
The Heart of Hanwi
Blood Tithe
End of the Line